Sierra —
You've truly given
us a gift with these
cookies — and your e...
tonight. thank you v...
Mackay

The Land of Godsdorf

STEVIE B. B. KING

Ciara,
Thank you for
the support! You
are amazing!!
Love,
[signature]

Sierra,
Your Joy and
happiness at your
reception to our book
was made me
Joyeous.
❤ ERIC

ISBN: 1984103563
ISBN-13: 978-1984103567

DEDICATION

To bears, humans, and bird-humans, without which this book would
be different.

CONTENTS

ACKNOWLEDGMENTS

We would like to acknowledge you, dear reader. You've gone further than 90% of the poor souls who pick up this book.

Best of luck, Godsdorfians.

Raban

The Mellori family did not fare well in their community. This is not to say that they were not fair folks or even quite successful folks, but rather, that they were not treated fairly by their community. In their neighbors' defense, the Melloris did not act like normal Arborns. To begin with, their nest did not look the others. Their family nest deviated from the standard Arborn design; their walls were neither thick nor sturdy nor disguised against the tree. Instead of using thick thuma branches and stacking them in crusty mud, the Melloris weaved an intricate pattern of bright emerald green reeds around their trunk to form a thin wall and used a soft paste of ruby red berries to nestle their reeds against the tree. While it proved to be sturdy enough for any thunderstorm, it appeared more artistic than utilitarian and natural. Their neighbors would wonder, and often out loud, if their family even belonged in the Arborn community.

However, this question did not phase the Melloris. They were accustomed to being outsiders in this community. Great grandmother, Rohima Mellori, one of the original Arborn tree nesters, was also one of the first in the family to draw the community's curiosity and scorn. Shortly after she moved into the trees, she started pursuing travels outside of the forest, only returning several times a year from excursions to the mountains. These non-Arborn desires for exploration pushed against the communal Arborn doctrines and, unfortunately, these impulses to leave the forests seemed to pass directly to her heirs. While most second generation Arborn families focused on building additions to their sturdy thuma nests, her children, Imma and Rete, started traveling to unknown areas around the Land of Godsdorf right after their Ceremony rites. They became the first successful Arborns to sail around the entire Inland bay, returning to the trees after five seasons with shells, seafood, and stories. This desire to travel in boats and explore outside of the trees made their family, in the gentlest terms, appear as misfits. While most Arborns considered this draw to explore foreign lands as unnatural, the knowledge the Melloris shared when they returned gave them a great degree of political power. Many other Arborns found their information about mountain resources, Inland towns, and weapon designs to be intriguing to say the least. Yet for the most part, they were left alone in their green and red nest in the corner of their town, Rooke, and for at least a while they had remained in that nest without too much movement.

So when Raban's parents, Rehassa and Urt, told him and his sister that they were going on an adventure outside the forest, he was not too surprised. However, his only disappointment was in the fact that he and his sister were not invited.

Raban did not know what to say when he first heard the news. He glanced over to his sister, Muni. She was sitting at their large thuma table. Her eyes were closed, and her long eyelashes were wet. Raban could not look away. In some ways, he was preparing for this moment his entire life. His parents had hinted at this upcoming absence for many years, and it was now finally realized. He stared at his crying sister. She was not ready for this moment at all—her chest heaved slowly as she tried to muffle her heavy sobs in her feathers. Raban's eyes shifted away. He was never good at consoling. He just sat across the table in silence, clenching down on his beak.

Their mother started first. Her pale face radiated from a sea of dark fluffy feathers. She stood a few steps away from the table in their main nesting space. Her beak quivered before she spoke.

"We never wanted to leave you two, but this must happen for the betterment of the community. It might seem sudden for us to leave, and we wanted to stay at least another week to see your Anting rite next week, Raban. But, due to unforeseen circumstances, we need to leave much sooner than we expected. We need to travel across the forest to Ringer's Bay."

Silence. Raban continued to sit there. He could hear Muni's continued muffled sobs, but all he could think about was how much he hated the taste of these thuma leaves. Their aftertaste lingered in the back of his throat. He pushed them in a small circle around his bowl repeatedly. Somehow, he hoped by doing so, it would appear as some form of eating.

He heard that Inlanders didn't have to eat these bitter things. Raban also heard that they grew all sorts of plants and ate different foods every day. He was envious. It was the third day in a row that their main meal was thuma leaves. No berries, no pine nuts, no tree worms; just raw crunchy thuma leaves. He wanted to remind his family that they were not caterpillars nor tree ants; they were not born for this diet. They were members of the great Mellori clan. Their clan was the first to climb Mt. Vesus, the first to round the Inland bay, and the first to eat raw Sealhorse! Yet Raban sat there in silence. This same pride gave Raban a deep sense of sadness. It was this same desire that drove his parents to leave him and his sister now. They were driven by their family impulse to travel and explore. They wanted to be the first to travel out on Ringer's Bay, he knew, and he sort of respected it.

"When do... you leave..." croaked Muni, in between hiccups. Her big tearful eyes opened wide and darted between their two parents.

Rehassa and Urt glanced at each other. Urt stepped forward this time but moved with heavy bones. Their father was barely a beak taller than their mother, but his presence was much greater. It was hard to maintain eye contact with him typically. Yet today his eyes appeared tired and soft.

9

STEVIE B. B. KING

"We will need to leave in the 'morrow, before sunrise... I know this sudden departure doesn't make much sense, and I know it all seems to be happening so fast. But you need to trust us... we will be back, and you will understand one day," replied their father.

His eyes turned down to look at Muni, but she did not look up. She laid her head down on the table and started to weep even louder than before. Raban continued to sit there in silence.

His mind was stuck on the thuma leaves. It astounded him that his whole family seemed to enjoy eating them. They were so bitter and so crunchy to him. He continued to push the leaves in a swirling pattern on his plate. Raban often wondered if other folks just pretended that they were sweet and tasty. Like everyone experienced the same horrible bitterness, but due to Arborn tradition and bravado, nobody would admit that they tasted bad. Whenever Raban chewed them they felt so stringy and dry, and then later, they gave him a burning sensation in the back of the throat when he tried to sleep. Was he alone in this experience? He picked up a few smaller ones and chewed them up. Their sharp tannic taste in his beak caused him to gag, and he spit them in a big wad on the floor beside the table.

"Raban! Please don't do that," called his mother. Raban glanced up at her; her body was stiff, and her short wings were crossed, but her face still seemed to glow. His stomach seemed to jump up into his throat. It hurt to swallow. *Damn thuma leaves*...Raban thought.

He stood up from the table and walked over to where he spit the leaves. He stopped behind his sister and rubbed Muni softly on the back. Her back feathers shuddered at first, but then she leaned into his support. Muni was strong for her young age, but she still had lots to grow. She was three years younger than him and was about half his height. Her feathers were still fleecy and short, but her mind had matured faster than her body. She had the heart of a Mellori, without ever experiencing the heartbreak that came with being one. Raban patted her on the head. She still had lots to learn, and Raban would have to be that family guide from now on.

Muni looked up at him. Her large eyes were glistening on her small round face. Her young face still had new grey feathers growing on it.

"Thanks, Rabe," said Muni. She looked just like their mom. His throat continued to heat up.

"Of course, Muni," Raban whispered.

"But what is going to happen to us?" Muni responded in a hushed tone so that their parents couldn't hear.

Raban's inner feathers twitched.

"Don't stress Muni. We will go over to Great Auntie's tomorrow. Don't you remember that she lives right by the Forest Edge? Where you can see all types of inland animals and you can pick all sorts of berries?

You're going to love that area," Raban replied in a hushed, but firm tone. It reminded him of his stoic father.

Neither of them had seen that area or their Great Auntie in many years, but Raban had one good memory of it.

He remembered his Great Auntie, Muni, and him all picking umma berries together around the Forest Edge many years ago, and his Great Auntie telling them to stop. As they peeked over the berry bush, they saw a magnificent Kascin Deer approaching. It was a big male, with massive sharp antlers, and piercing white stripes. Not fully grown but separate from its pack. Raban locked eyes with it, and it bowed to them, and walked away. It was a calming memory tonight.

Muni let out a large sigh, but she was no longer crying. Raban felt relief and a sudden surge of exhaustion. He knew it was time to wrap things up for the night, so he gave Muni a side-wing hug, and patted her on the head one more time. He then walked over to their parents. They both were still standing; both had their wings crossed.

Raban was not sure what to do. His throat was hot, and his stomach seemed to not enjoy all those thuma leaves. He picked up the thuma leaves that he spit and gave his parents a small bow. When he looked back up, neither of his parents had their wings crossed.

"Oh Raban, you will never know how much we care about you. We know this isn't a good time to leave, but you must understand, we have no choice..." burst out his mother. She swooped her wings around him and squeezed.

When she let go, his father had wiped his tears away. He walked over and rested both of his hands on Raban's shoulders. They were heavy and wrapped over his entire shoulder feathers. He looked down at Raban with his grey blue eyes and spoke in thick words.

"You are about to have your maturity rites, and I will not be there to guide you as I hoped. But the rites will happen regardless... and I know I've never said this, but you are ready for them. Do not overthink it like your friends. You are a Mellori boy, you were born for this. You are destined for a special path." His father turned away walked over to their short corner stool. Raban swallowed hard again. His face was on fire.

"I also want you to have this." His father handed him a massive talon. He had never seen a Corvidean talon this size before. He looked down at his own talons, and this one looked at least four times the size. There was a string tied around it, and the string was woven from some type of light hair that he had never seen before.

Raban held it in his hand and flipped it over. There was no animal that he could think of that would have this size talon, and the hair was taut but silky.

"What is this?" asked Raban, his small eyebrow feathers raised.

"It is an old family heirloom. It's been in the Mellori clan since before the Settling. We, Mellori, have always passed it down to the next in line to lead the family. I was waiting to give it to you after the Ceremony, but I think fate has decided to hasten life... I don't have time tonight to tell you more about the necklace, but I know in time, it will reveal itself to you."

Raban was confused but could not take his eyes off the talon. It's dark obsidian curved edge, and its sharp point shined in the fire's light. It had an odd circular red marking on the base of it and a few other small red scratches radiating around it. He held it close to his body and Raban could almost feel it vibrate. It seemed to beckon him to put it on. He looked back at his father, who had a weak smile on, and nodded at Raban. He saw Muni admiring his new family token. Tears were no longer in her eyes, but a sense of excitement. Raban put the necklace carefully over his neck. The talon rested on top of his chest feathers. His throat had finally stopped hurting. He had a sudden feeling that Muni and he were going to be just fine.

Luteo

It suddenly dawned on Luteolus that the forest had fallen silent — no whistling sparrows in the canopy or ruffed grouse pecking in the lower ferns. The usual cacophony of the woods was replaced by a deafening and ominous stillness that seemed to freeze time itself and suck the air from his lungs. Luteo raised his head from the overripe dogwood berries that he had been collecting and scanned the tree-line directly ahead. The weave of branches and undergrowth looked as it always had, the scene exactly as it had appeared moments earlier. Luteo sniffed the air, finding the usual scents of pine and hemlock woven above the damp undertones of silt and clay. Perplexed, he lowered his head and continued stripping the ruby-red globes from the dogwood with his furry brown paws, funneling the berries into his rucksack. *After years of harvesting and helping Father with the apples, I'm only one bushel away from the next chapter of my life,* Luteo thought. *This is a day I'm going to remember for the rest of my life — the end of an era.* Smiling to himself, Luteo flipped a handful of berries into his mouth and moved onto the next dogwood.

Snap! Luteo jerked his head upward and whipped his snout to the right, just in time to register a blurry shape careening towards his back. Diving to the left, Luteo twisted in the air to catch the projectile on his left breast and was rewarded with a wet punch to his chest.

"Another point for me, Luteo!" a voice yelled from the bushes.

Luteo looked down at the rotten apple pulp on his fur, and jumped to his feet, brushing off the mealy apple core and seeds.

"Pern, you Den-filth! I see you back there. Show your face!"

A light brown head appeared above the brush-line, with a toothy grin spanning from ear to ear. The bear started cantering towards Luteo, barely making a sound as he parted the bushes with his paws.

"You make it easier and easier on me," Pern scoffed. "You need to keep your focus on your surroundings and constantly check for any dangers, just like Kermodei keeps telling you!"

"Shut up," Luteo growled as he rose to his feet. "I was busy trying to collect the last of the dogwoods this season. What did you manage to gather today during your breaks from disturbing other folks?" Luteo grinned.

Pern lumbered up to Luteo as he rose and brushed the dried leaves and twigs from his back-fur.

"I've been out past Agronomist Dolinensis' crop, rounding up the last of the morels and thimble-caps. I think we're already the last few out here," Pern said, "so can we head home already? I'm dying to say goodbye to Pruin and tonight's the last night in a while where we can still be with our family."

Luteo checked his belongings to make sure he still had much of his harvest within his rucksack and looked down at Pern.

"Alright, you cub-brain," Luteo chuckled. "Let's go turn our crop into Berarbor's stores and spend some time with our folks." He grabbed Pern's shoulder and turned him around while grappling his arm in a square-lock. "That is, if you can escape my grip without tapping out!"

"You're on!" Pern rumbled, while twisting up and into Luteo's arms.

***

Despite being born and raised in Berarbor, the towering oak and maple eldertrees never failed to send a shiver down Luteo's spine. Luteo and Pern made their way to Berarbor's main gate and entrance to the central trunk, following the well-worn cobblestoned road that supported the flow of Ursa into and out of the city. Berarbor's size was deceptive. Any arriving creature might first register the skyline of Berarbor from a few clicks out and think little of it – only to find during the subsequent approach that the eldertrees seem to keep looming larger and larger until they blot out the very sun and sky.

Surrounded by a relatively young forest that had barely graced a few millennia on Godsdorf, the age of the eldertrees that supported Berarbor on their mighty boughs were lost to time itself. *"While it is known the Ursa have inhabited these lands for the last few epochs, we are only left with oral history to try to piece together our founding of Berarbor over 10,000 seasons ago,"* Luteo remembered Kermodei lecturing during his history lessons in the Institute. *While Ursolympa might be the wealthiest of the kingdens, and Terrarctos the largest, Berarbor is most certainly the oldest.* Luteo had yet to see another kingden but found it hard to imagine one larger or richer than his home.

"Where does your mind wander when your eyes glaze over like that?" Pern asked as he stopped mid-stride and prodded Luteo in his arm.

Luteo turned his gaze from the lofty households nestled in the branches of Berarbor down to his stout brother-in-season.

"I'm just trying my best to remember how Berarbor looks and feels and smells so I can return to this brief second after we leave for the Liberalia. I've spent every waking moment in this kingden and I can't imagine being away from it." Expecting to hear the usual jibe or guffaw from Pern, Luteo was surprised to see a reverent smile slowly grow on Pern's face.

"You are such a romantic, Luteo. The funny thing is, I think I know exactly what you mean." Pern turned his head up to the eldertrees and continued his slow walk. "I remember learning how to swim and chase salmon out past Agronomist Lira's pastures, before we snuck into his stores and helped ourselves to some of his blackberry preserve. He always managed to age it just right, so the acidity of the berries perfectly balanced the sugar from the juice."

Luteo grinned and kept pace with Pern. "If I recall correctly, it was *you* who did the sneaking."

"Minor details." Pern chortled. "It's easier to ask for forgiveness than for permission. Besides, you've gotten fat on a lot of my 'sneakings' so you had better watch out before you bite the hand that feeds you."

"Enough of your aphorisms, Pern. You can keep your pennies and your thoughts." Luteo teased.

Luteo and Pern approached the ornamental gate recessed into the main trunk of Berarbor. Flanked by two sets of Denguards in full battle armor, the bronze gateway slowly parted to allow enough room for the two Ursa to make their way into the hollowed central trunk. The usually bustling hearth of Berarbor was unusually quiet as the last day of harvest was traditionally one that the Ursa spent with their families, before welcoming the winter and start of a new season. Luteo and Pern made their way across the cavernous hall to the staircases lining the outer wall of the trunk. Twenty-five flights of stairs and around ten minutes later, the duo emerged panting into the Main Square of Central Berarbor.

"Normally I found Liberalia's Eve to be a relaxing and peaceful time," Luteo said as he slowly surveyed the empty square, "but it's a different story when it's *our* Liberalia. I just want everything to be as I remember it until we have to leave."

"You and I used to help hang these banners and stock the picnic tables back when we were 11 seasons old." Pern ran his paw over the covered tables lining the perimeter of the Main Square. "27 seasons seemed so old and wise back then. But I barely feel like I've aged since then." A breeze carrying the first chill of winter wound its way through the dwellings surrounding the square and gave Luteo a shiver that was only partly due to the temperature.

"I guess we're going to have to grow up quickly", Luteo said as he locked eyes with Pern.

Naka

Naka woke to the sound of the rooster's crow. The early light had already crept its way onto his mat, and even for these warm months it was bright. He had overslept. He sighed as he rose to his feet, tied his mapa around his waist, and walked into the larger family room in the center of the house. As usual, his dad and grandmother were already gone. By now his dad would be well on his way to the edges of the reef, where the surf broke and the most expensive fish could be found. His obachan, as he had called his grandmother since he could talk, would already be at the village center, weaving with most of the other men and women of her age.

Naka navigated between houses and people, careful to avoid getting in the way of any elders, until he came to a stream a few hundred yards away. Once at the stream, he turned and walked alongside it, opposite the stream's flow. He let the sand press between his toes with each step. When he reached a thatched house much like his own, he approached the entryway and announced his presence. Having heard no response, he wiped his feet on the woven mat just outside the door and entered. He had told Kane yesterday that he'd meet him at his house, but he must have woken up even later than he thought. He left the house and quickened his pace toward the fields.

Kane spotted him as he approached the rice pond and waved. "I thought you may have forgotten what you said yesterday and left straight for the fields. Did you sleep in?" asked Kane once Naka came within reasonable earshot. "Yeah, I woke up with the sun already at my waist. I think I need a new rooster," he complained with a smile. Kane gave him a courtesy chuckle. The daze from having recently woken up hadn't made Naka any funnier. "How long have you been working?"

"Oh, not too long. I've only gone through the first row."

Naka nodded and then sloshed into the pond and got to work. This far into the season, it wasn't much longer before the draining and the harvesting could begin, but for now the wet and dirty work of weeding needed doing. Most of the other farmers referred to this time period as the wading season, but Naka always thought waiting season fit better to the work. The task of planting the seeds and filling the ponds had long since ended, and now all there was to do was keep doing the maintenance work at hand and hope that you got your crops off to a good enough start and kept them happy enough that you got a good haul when the harvest came around. Before he had passed, Naka's grandfather would compare the cycle to raising Naka's dad and aunts: a lot of work, preparation, and planning upfront, followed by much more time waiting, trying to be responsive to problems and dangers as you see them, and finally, when the kid reached adulthood, finding out what sort of person that kid became.

Naka didn't have any kids—although some of his peers did—so he had only his own life to compare it to. It seemed to him that life involved some amount of preparing and planning, followed by a lot of waiting and pulling out weeds where you could see them, before finally getting to a point where you could take a step back, see what your efforts had yielded, and try to harvest as much of that as you could.

He moved from row to row, arching down to pull weeds from the root as he saw them. He worked on the other side of the rice pond from Kane in one of the square plots allotted to their families so that when they met in the middle they could call it a day. Today though, Naka would let Kane stop working a little before that point to make up for his tardiness.

Since they started at opposite ends of the pond, the mornings typically did not lead to much conversation, although the two whistled and sang when the mood struck them. Naka liked the reflective periods that the mornings offered, especially before the sun reached its highest point and the work got that much more exhausting.

It had been a hot summer so far, and the extra warmth from the sun had required the workers to divert extra water from the streams to the rice field. The rice farmers in the village, including Naka and Kane, depended on the flow of water through the village—water that came down from the peaks of the mountains far to the east. Mountains that Naka couldn't even see from where he stood. Not only the rice farmers relied on the water, too. The water ran through these rice fields and took with it precious nutrients in its path downstream to the fish ponds where koi farmers raised and caught their livelihoods. The rice ponds themselves played host to a variety of critters, including crayfish that Naka liked to bring home to add to supper on special occasions.

He had worked for just over half the day when a man's low voice called out to him.

"I didn't see you here with the sun today, Naka." Naka turned to face the voice's owner, though he could have placed that voice with his eyes shut. As expected, Boto Nishimoto's face stared back at him with its typical mixture of disgust and condescension. Naka bowed deeply as a sign of respect for the overseer of his rice ponds.

"Yes, Boto, I arrived a little after the sun today. I think I need a new rooster."

Boto did not take as kindly to the joke as Kane had.

"This is the second time you've been late this season, Naka. Tell me, do you care about your work? Do you want these crops to thrive? Do you want a great yield that strengthens Sokoku and brings your family the praise of the Empress? Do you want to earn respect for yourself?"

Naka stared down at him. "Yes, sir."

"Then I wonder why you do not act like it? I would think that your Yamahito side would make you a better, more diligent worker despite your Nakai blood. Tell me, how did you manage to get the worst attributes of both sides of your heritage? The pride of the Yamahito with the laziness of the Nakai is not a winning combination."

Naka said nothing, careful not to let his face betray the anger he felt swelling up inside.

"Well?" Boto continued. "Do you have an answer for me?"

"I do not know," said Naka.

"No surprise there. Do not be late again. The next time you're late I'll increase the tariffs on your yields by 30%. See to it that your work is finished today." Boto smirked at his threat and strolled away to find more prey at another section of pond.

"Tell me," mimicked Naka once Boto was out of earshot. "How is it that he can be so small a person and still such a huge dick at the same time?"

"He really lives up to his name, doesn't he?" Kane replied.

Naka laughed. "He really does."

Boto wasn't a common first name for the Yamahito, but it was common enough not to raise any eyebrows in the mountains or even in the wooded hills that spanned the distance between the mountains and the coast. Out closer to the ocean though, in Nakai districts, the name had a more phallic connotation. Whenever Boto would come by and badger Naka and Kane, Naka took in a great deal of satisfaction in the knowledge that he must have spent years up in the mountain towns studying and working and schmoozing to achieve his cushy overseer position just to end up assigned to the coast, where in private the mere mention of his name sparked laughter even among the older folk. Naka wondered whether Boto had made an enemy in the wrong place somewhere along the way who knew that his name would cost him some small measure of respect and authority among those he was meant to supervise.

Still, Boto deserved the comparison. Land overseers were known for their strict rules and generous interpretation of the powers granted to them, but Boto took it to another level. He acted like he owned the land under his purview. Not only was that not true even under Yamahito law, as overseers did not own land, the very concept of ownership contradicted the natural state of things. This land belonged to the Nakai people, to people like Kane, like Naka's father and grandmother, and like the village elders that the younger folks called aunt and uncle. The land belonged to the newest children of the community, and to the eldest folk approaching their last sunrise in this life. The gods gave the Nakai this land, and it would never belong to Boto, or to his people, just like it would never belong to Naka—at least not completely.

Naka finished up the last few rows of the day while Kane sat at the water's edge, taking advantage of his earlier start. The two talked and laughed and sang for those last several minutes of the day, and as the sun was beginning to set they packed up and made the walk back to the village.

Raban

Raban awoke to the sound of water pattering overhead. It was spring rain, no longer the winter mists of yestermonth. The steady, slow drops sounded like birds dancing on the nest-top, their little talons tapping all over the tight woven reeds. Raban did not feel like waking up, but he knew if they did not start packing soon, they would never reach the Forest Edge by nightfall.

He grabbed the edges of his hammock and lifted his weary body up. Last night still felt surreal to him.

"What is this thing?" Raban thought as he clutched the large talon that hung from his chest. It felt even bigger than he remembered.

Was it a real family heirloom? What type of talon was that? Were his parents leaving for good? Why could they not just stay in their family house? Wasn't he about to become a full-grown Arborn in a week? Would Great Auntie even remember Muni and him?

These questions and more kept fluttering across Raban's mind as he wandered around the cold and hollow nest. Its woven floor crinkled under his feet. He started packing up anything that made sense to bring to Great Auntie's. At first, he gathered his personal items like his bone-carved feather comb, his copper beak cleaner, his iron carving knife, and his newly-acquired talon necklace, and wrapped them all together in his hammock. He then proceeded to gather some of their other family gear. He grabbed his mother's Huginn Holy Book; it was marvelous to behold. She would only bring it out for special holy days, and for the Years' End Gathering. Today, it was left out on the table, as a clear reminder for them to take it with them.

As he pushed the book into his sack, he walked over to his parents' sleeping corridor. On their hammock, rested his mother's bow made of rare Bue wood, and her iron-tipped arrows, a rare sight in the Arborn community. Iron weapons were more of an Inlander specialty. Their mother had been one of the finest bow shots in Arborn. Her arrows always had such impeccable accuracy, their neighbors often forgot to invite her to shooting competitions. Without her to train Raban, he was not sure if he would pass the Ceremony shooting exercises, but nevertheless, he packed the bow in his bag.

Finally, he gathered up his father's other tools and weapons, including his small pack of poison-tipped throwing darts, a dangerous oddity that his ancestors picked up somewhere along Inlander's bay. He also grabbed his father's old Guardian polespear, a relic from the Inlander past, and made from high-quality Bue wood and iron tipped. It was one of the most dangerous weapons a Corvidean could have, when wielded by a trained spear dancer or spear thrower. He had seen his father hit a target from nearly three thuma-tree lengths away with it. The sharp iron spearhead could pierce right through thick thuma shields with ease. The fact that he had left his most powerful weapon here for Raban was surprising. While Raban did train under his father to throw and dance with the spear, he assumed that his father would need it on his parents' mysterious journey.

Finally, he reached over and grabbed his father's thick waterskin. His father claimed that this water jug was impenetrable to even steel and that it was made from the bladder of a Giant River Otter. These legendary beasts were known to eat Corvidians whole when they attacked. Their stomachs were able to digest feather, bones, and all. Having a waterskin that could not rip would be a great travel tool.

With all these items, and a handful of valuable ancient coins, he stuffed as much as he could carry on his back, swung the waterskin over his left wing, and carried the polespear in his right hand. He was ready.

There was a knock on the outside door upstairs. Raban put his gear down in a pile and headed up to see who was there. He peeked through the slit in the entrance reeds. It was Navine!

"Ka'kaw, the notorious Navey has returned. Welcome back!" said Raban as he pushed up the reed door.

"Ka'kaw, Rabe! And thanks…." Navine looked a little flush in her face and avoided eye contact with Raban. Her wings were dripping wet.

"Oh, come off it Navey, how long have we known each other? It's not that big of a deal about the Ceremony," replied Raban.

"So, you have heard… I would hope there would be more privacy when it comes to these holy rites, but what do I know," said Navine as she scratched the soft wet wood floor mindlessly with one of her big talons.

"It's not even a big deal; I heard that you bowed out of the Anting ritual, but that you'll try again next week at the same time as my Anting rite. So, if anything it's a good thing! We will be there to support each other," Raban said with a wink.

"Hah! That is one way of looking at it…. My neighbors seem to think differently. I hear them whispering that I don't belong in the trees, and that I should go farm with the Inlanders."

"Are you kidding me, Navey? I've seen you wrestle ground boars! Hell, I've even seen you bite the head off a full-grown tree rat! You're stronger than most full-grown Corvideans, and anyone who thinks otherwise doesn't know Huginn"

Navine's face flushed bright red. "Well thanks Rabe, but I think that is a minority opinion in the community right now. I overheard one Huginn monk say that it was the first time he's seen someone fail the Anting rite this season, but that he wasn't surprised it was a female youngling." She glanced up at Rabe, and there was a shot of fire in her eyes.

"Navey, I didn't know you converted! Because why else are you suddenly listening to the words of Huginn monks?" Rabe asked with a smile.

Navine's hard shell cracked a little, and she laughed. It was the first time her beak smiled since coming over. Raban felt a little burn in the back of his throat.

"Fair point, Rabe. Fair point. Honestly, the whole thing was stupid. I mean what do they even expect to learn from the rite. Arborns are all about following tradition and ritual, but I think most people are as confused by them as me."

"I agree with you there, Navey. People here do things because they think they have to," Raban said as he thought about his parent's defense of their trip. "But for better or worse, it's a small, superstitious community. Word spreads about anything and everything. Soon enough, my sister and I will be the ones that people are talking about, and your whole ritual debacle will be a story of yesterday!"

"We do always find something new to distract us—but wait, what do you mean about you and your sister?"

"Well my parents left this morning to head to the other side of the forest to sail around Ringer's Bay."

"Ringer's Bay!? What in Huginn's name are they doing that for?" Navine asked. Her eyes leaped opened.

"Oh, you know, in the Mellori family tradition, I assume my parents want to be the first to go there… but honestly, they did not explain much about it before they left."

"Wow, you're right, you guys will be the talk of the town! I mean, I'm not sure what to say Rabe. I don't mean it like that. I'm really sorry to hear that they are leaving…" She glanced down at the ground and started drawing circles with her big talon again.

"Nothing to be sorry about; my sister and I will move in with my Great Auntie for a while on the Forest Edge. It will be fine. It's almost Umma berry season too, and they will be quite plentiful out in those parts. Also, I can still travel back and forth to Rooke. It's only a half day's journey."

"The Forest Edge? You will be very close to the Inlanders though. I've heard people still see some city guards patrolling near there. Do you think you will be safe out there?"

"City guards in the forests? I guess you really do listen to the tales of Huginn monks!" Rabe laughed.

"Hey! I heard that directly from my cousin. The city guards wander near there. I'm serious. They would never enter the forest, but still something to know, I guess, especially when you are with Muni."

"Well I will keep that in mind, Navey. And thanks again for stopping by. It was great to see you. Right now, I need to finish packing up and then check on my sister, but I will see you in a few suns for our Anting rite, hopefully we both can be the talk of the town on how great we do!"

"Oh, don't worry, I wouldn't mind not being talked about for a while, but good luck on your journey, and see you then!" Navine waved. As she turned away, her eyes stayed on Raban.

"We've got this, Navey! See you soon!"

Raban closed the door. His heart was shaking his chest. It was good to see Navine.

He headed back down the mossy steps to his sister's sleeping corridor. He peeked inside, half expecting her to be still asleep. Instead, her space was cleaned out of all her valuables; she was packed and ready to go. Raban was proud of her and his parents for training them so well.

"Ka'kaw, ready to go, Muni?" Raban asked, knowing her answer already.

"Yes, Rabe, all packed and ready to go!" replied Muni. Her eyes looked determined, but there was a wall of innocence behind them.

"Well mother and father are gone, and I've packed everything else we need. We better get moving if we want to make it there by nightfall."

Muni nodded, and grabbed her small pack and swung it around her shoulder. They walked back over to his pile of gear.

"Okay good, but before we go, I want to make sure we have some ground rules. You remember that you are my little sister, right? And that you will need to listen to me now that mother and father are gone, even when we are at Great Auntie's? No matter what I ask, it's always in your best interest to listen to me, okay? Does that make sense?"

"Of course, Rabe, I will always listen to you!" said Muni with a wry smile on her face. She did a slight bow to him.

Raban chuckled. "Well, at least we have that settled. So, to start with, you are on water duty for the entire trip" said Raban, as he handed over their father's waterskin to Muni.

"You will be responsible for carrying the water, refilling the water, and protecting the water jug. This could be an issue of life and death. Do you understand that?" asked Raban, trying his best to channel their father's spirit. He felt like this was a small job for Muni but a very important one.

Muni did not say anything, but she seemed to understand the seriousness of it and nodded. She hung the water jug around her left wing.

She also held their great-grandmother's walking staff in her right hand. She looked like a little adventurer; like a real Mellori.

As they stepped outside their family's nest onto its foundation branch, the rain slowed down a little. Raban took a deep breath. The air was sharp; he could feel his lungs shiver. He did not enjoy the rain, but today, it felt fitting. The cold heavy spring drops rolled off his shoulders as he gripped his polespear and walked across the branch. It was nice having the spear. The heavy pole in his hand helped balance the weight on his back. Raban did not want to imagine what would happen if one of them slipped off the treeline.

After walking from their nesting-tree branch, they reached the two hanging bridges. The one to his right was the one they always walked down. The wood planks even seemed to have grooves for his talon steps. This bridge led them into Rooke's town square, it led them to the Gathering, it led them to all their friends and fellow community members. The pathway to the left was rarely used. This bridge led them to the west, to the Forest Edge, to the Inland, to the Forbidden Mountains, to the unknown. It was the path less traveled, but today, it would be their route.

Muni must have slept well because without hesitation, she started walking down the left bridge, and not just walking, but leading Raban down the path. She used the walking staff like a ninth talon, propelling herself faster than she normally walked. The bridge swayed as she pushed the staff down onto it. When Raban peered over the edge, he was amazed how high up they were.

The tree bridges were still a modern phenomenon to Raban. Before these hanging things were built to connect the trees, the Arborns had relied on rope swings, wing gliding, and ladders to move from one tree to the next. These original methods were unpredictable and dangerous, especially at night. Raban used to hear about all sorts of accidents; it was not uncommon for some older folks to be hurt or even killed by slipping off the ropes or slamming into an unseen tree branch after dusk. The bridges reduced the amount of accidents, but things could still happen on these wet wooden planks. Raban made sure to watch whether Muni's steps stayed in the center of the path.

After reaching the third tree on their route, Muni stopped at the trunk, sat down, and gulped down some water from their jug. She looked a bit winded, but her eyes were smiling.

"Rabe, don't you love these tree bridges? They make me feel like a real bird moving from tree to tree over the groundfloor with ease," Muni said with a dreamy look on her face.

"Sure, in a way, Muni. But you must remember that we are walking from tree to tree. It's going to take us a long time to get to the Forest Edge."

"I know, but it just feels so freeing, like we are connected to that part of ourselves so much more. Even if it takes a while to get to Great Auntie's, we are hovering over the ground the whole time, which is quite bird-like!"

"I guess that is true Muni, and we could even glide for part of the way if we wanted, but we would hit the ground soon and have to walk once again…. We cannot fly, Muni, and you know that. This hovering over the ground is just an illusion. No matter what you've heard at our Gatherings, we are not actually birds. The Huginn monks forget that sometimes."

Muni did not appreciate this type of criticism. Her face twisted, and she gulped down some more water. She was young and believed things hard.

"But, Rabe, we are part bird. And like they say at the Gatherings, Corvideans that deny this fact, like you, either fail to remember that heritage or are just scared of our own greatness!"

"Yes, Muni, I fail to remember that fact," said Raban, as he waved his wing feathers in the air.

"And don't think that I'm afraid that we have wings, I just don't want you to get caught up in all of this Huginn religious rubbish. I think it is extreme. There is no doubt that part of it is true, but we are not very different from the Inlanders, we have human ancestry, as well."

Muni did not look convinced, but she nodded along and sipped more at the water. She started to hum a Gathering song.

"Well, Muni, feel free to embrace your inner bird and fly the rest of the way. I'll just meet you there. But if not, let's start walking. We still have a long way to go, and I don't want to travel after the sunset." Raban nudged her with the soft end of his polespear. "Also, let me have a few sips of that water before you drink the whole thing!"

She shook her head, ruffling her feathers and handed him the jug. It was much lighter than he expected; he took a few conservative sips and gave it back. At this rate, they would probably need to stop and refill from a waterhole on a Bue tree soon.

Luteo

Throwing off his thick wool cloak and shaking his matted fur, Luteo shut the door behind him and placed his knapsack onto the entryway table. The familiar scents of allspice and linen wafted over him and he took a deep breath of warm air into his lungs, expelling all his worries and anxiety with any last remnants of the frigid late-fall air.

"Is that you, Luteolus?" a voice called from inside the house.

"Yes, Mother. I've brought some of the last dogwood berries and managed to snag some of the morels that Pern collected."

"Wonderful!" A brown paw streaked with grey reached out from behind the doorframe leading into the living room, gesturing with an open palm. "Hand me those morels, would you? I'll add them to the cream sauce. This is my last chance to give you a home-cooked meal, and I'm going to do my best."

Luteo licked his lips, digging through his rucksack and handing the mushrooms to his mother. He followed his mother's retreating hand into the living room and felt a wave of heat from the fireplace radiating warmth into the room. Carved directly into the ancient bark of the eldertrees, the entire home was insulated from the outside weather and provided a welcome respite from the bitter winds that whipped through the upper reaches of Berarbor. Their living room was modest but well-planned, with comfortably worn furniture and a thick wool carpet that heated even the coldest of paws.

"Lu!" a little voice chirped from the far side of the living room. Isabell looked up from her picture book and jumped up. "You're back from the woods! Tell me all about it. Did you see any Ursa coming from the other kingdens?"

Luteo chuckled as he sat and sunk into the deep cushions of his favorite armchair. Isabell launched herself from the carpet, and he sunk further backwards into the chair as she sat on his lap.

"You're getting too old for this. Are you turning seven this season?" Luteo grabbed the wooden brush from the side table and started working out the knots in Isabell's fine fleece.

Isabell settled into her reading while taking up the majority of Luteo's lap, and he brushed her fur while letting his mind wander. The smells of his mother's cooking slowly drifted into the living room and fused with the smells he associated with his childhood. Soon Luteo's eyelids started to grow heavy and he found himself slipping in and out of consciousness.

"Wake up, son."

Luteo picked up his slumped head from his chest and rubbed the sleep from his eyes. He opened his eyes to see his father standing over him, with his paw placed on Luteo's shoulder. The fire had died down, and the room was slightly darker and colder. Isabell had disappeared, likely in her room playing with her model figurines.

"Now we can't let you spend your last night with the family snoozing away, can we?" he chuckled playfully and tousled Luteo's fur behind his ears. Just like most Ursa at his father's age, his fur was just beginning to turn brighter, with streaks of bone-white highlighting his eyebrows and jawline. It gave him a distinguished look that was softened by the twinkle in his eye.

Luteo stood and cracked his back to get the blood flowing back into his legs and arms.

"Did I miss dinner?" Luteo questioned as his stomach rumbled.

"Do you really think we could eat without the Ursa of honor?" his father replied. Although his father was smiling, Luteo noticed that his father's eyes didn't match his grin.

"Before we eat, I need to speak with you." His father placed his paw on Luteo's shoulder, only slightly lower than his own. His father looked directly into Luteo's eyes as he spoke.

"Tomorrow is a big day for you. The Liberalia is a time where each cub can shed the burden of youth and come into their own as an adult. It's not an easy trial. I remember some Ursa who didn't make it through the season." His father looked past Luteo suddenly, his eyes a thousand clicks away. "Above all you've got to watch over yourself. Watch over Pern. I won't be there to watch over you anymore, and you're going to have to do it alone now."

Luteo scanned his father's grave face and put his paw on his father's chest.

"I will, dad. I'm ready and I've been preparing for this day since I could walk."

His father's eyes suddenly re-focused, and he was back in the room with Luteo.

"I know, son. I know," he chuckled. "You've got to forgive my solemnity. I just worry about you. Now let's get you into the kitchen so you can help your mother put the finishing touches on your last decently cooked meal. You won't believe the gruel they call food during the Liberalia."

Luteo's father clasped his arm around Luteo's shoulder and steered him towards the door next to the fireplace. Luteo looked up at his father and walked into the heated kitchen.

***

Luteo leaned back into his chair and belched.

"Eww Lu. That's so gross." Isabell protested loudly. Luteo placed his paws on his stuffed stomach and hummed in a contented manner. His mother shook her head while Luteo saw his father try to hide his smirk behind a swig from his stein. Luteo could still taste the thick cream sauce on his tongue, could still smell the tart aroma of crispy salmon skin. The perfect send-off feast had been finished, and he felt very satisfied.

"Thank you, mother. I couldn't ask for a better goodbye gift." Luteo lowered his voice, trying to mimic his voice when he was a cub.

"You're welcome, son." His mother's eyes softened, and her smile returned to her face.

A loud and rapid knock echoed through their home. Luteo jerked upward in his chair and looked to his father.

"Now who could that be at this hour? On Liberalia's Eve no less?"

Luteo jumped to his feet and strode to the front door. He was unable to see anyone from the stained-glass window in the wooden door, and cracked it open slightly. A burst of icy wind blew the door open further, and Luteo was pushed back into the hallway. His hip caught on the entryway table holding his rucksack and he spilled backwards, falling onto his butt. A dark shape loomed over him backlit by the full moon behind it.

A feeling of dread slowly came over Luteo as the figure came closer and knelt over him. A bone white paw shot out from the obscured layers in the figure's mantle and grasped Luteo's forearm. To his amazement, the figure pulled Luteo upright.

"I'm sorry to frighten you my dear boy." A familiar voice spoke from beneath the cloak layers.

"Kermodei?" Luteo sputtered, pulling himself together. The figure pulled the cloak's hood backwards and unwrapped the scarf from his face. Kermodei's bone white shone from underneath the last few layers of scarf, and soon the teacher stood unmasked in Luteo's foyer.

"Yes, yes. I've been making the rounds making sure each youngling is ready for the Liberalia tomorrow. You were the last on my list, and I'm sorry for intruding so late on the Eve." Kermodei deposited his shed layers onto the table and looked expectantly at Luteo. Luteo paused for a second, still in a state of confusion.

"Ahem. Would you let me warm up by your hearth?" Kermodei cleared his throat and asked with a slight tinge of annoyance while looking down his snout at Luteo.

"Of course!" Luteo stiffened and stepped back to allow his mentor into the living room. Kermodei strode into the living room where Luteo's family was standing with varying states of perplexity. The tension exited the room as they recognized the friendly face, and Isabell came out from behind her father's legs.

"Uncle Kermy!" Isabell shouted and bounded towards him. Kermodei reached out with his frail paw and stopped Isabell in her tracks with an upheld paw.

"Hold on my dearest. Please let me warm my brittles bones as I'm inclined to believe they might snap in this turbid chill." Kermodei chided Isabell with a lighthearted air. Isabell looked at her toes with a dark shade of red blooming on her furry cheeks. She ran back to her story book which was in a neat pile near the hearth and stuck her head in the pages, trying to disappear from reality itself.

Kermodei chuckled, and took his time getting settled into the armchair closest to the now-roaring fire. Once gathering his robes about him, he gestured to Luteo for him to sit on the floor at his side.

Luteo looked at his parents, who still stood awkwardly by the kitchen door, and followed Kermodei's unspoken command. As he sat on the thick carpet, his father cleared his throat.

"Why don't we start washing the dishes, dear?" Placing his paw on mother's shoulder, Luteo's father guided both of them into the kitchen.

Kermodei sat in silence, seeming to relish the warmth and comfort of the fire. Luteo waited and tried to be patient, expecting Kermodei to soon explain the intrusion. A minute passed, and then five, before Luteo started to fidget. Isabell had forgotten her moment of embarrassment and was humming beneath her breath while flipping through her book. Luteo admired his sister's resiliency and unconditional optimism, and let a small smile come across his face.

"We do all this for them, you know?" Kermodei sat unmoving in his armchair, and Luteo was unsure from where the voice came. Luteo thought he saw Kermodei sit up in his periphery but kept his eyes on Isabell.

"The Liberalia has been a cornerstone of the Ursa as long as we can remember. The ritual is symbolic, yes, but it is also one of great practicality. How do you imagine we educate our youth in the ways of the hardness of life? It's easy to convey in words the blistering chill of winter and the isolation one feels when separated from their kin. Conversely, it's near impossible to register the gravity of what that moment feels like when surrounded by the amenities our kingden provides us.

"I'm convinced the single greatest threat to the Ursa is the inability of children to feel the wounds of their parents. We must inevitably relive our worst moments to rediscover our best strengths. And this cycle must repeat itself, over and over and over, until we find a way to remedy our perpetual amnesia. Like the droplet that must let itself be thrown down a waterfall, we are forever destined to learn what we already know, teach what has already been taught."

Kermodei paused, letting his words fade into the silent room. Luteo was captivated by Kermodei's ramblings and stared directly at his mentor's eyes while trying to decipher the chaotic thoughts that flashed beneath. Kermodei eye's flickered off the fire and met his gaze, sending a jolt through Luteo's spine.

"Tomorrow will be a day you never forget. For better or worse, tomorrow will give you a choice – to either embrace the knowledge of your fathers or find your own way in the night."

The crackling of the fire was the only sound hanging in the living room air. Kermodei's somber frown lingered for a moment, and then was gone.

"And with that, I take my leave."

Kermodei pulled himself into an upright position, leaning heavily on the armchair to steady himself. Luteo bounded upwards and grabbed his tutor's arm, guiding him towards the door.

"Master Kermodei..." Luteo began. Kermodei paused from wrapping his scarves around neck and shoulders.

"Worry not, Master Luteolus. You will overcome this trial if you remain true to yourself and to what we've learned during our time together." Kermodei smiled with an unusual air of satisfaction. "Spend tonight with your family. Enjoy those you love and love those whose company you enjoy."

With a torrent of cold wind Kermodei disappeared into the darkness outside. Luteo stood shell-shocked in the foyer, unsure of exactly what had just transpired. Had Kermodei been warning him to listen to the direction of his elders? Or warning against following the words before him blindly?

"Lu?" Isabell stood next to the living room doorframe and looked up at her big brother. "What was Kermodei talking about?"

Luteo looked down at his sister's questioning face and smiled.

"Who knows? Maybe Uncle Kermodei has gotten into Agronomist Pesso's mead again?" Isabell giggled and ran up to Luteo, giving him a big hug.

"I love you Lu. I'm going to miss you while you're gone."

"I'm going to miss you too."

Naka

The aroma of grandma's cooking commanded a radius of a dozen yards that night and had Naka and Kane salivating as they approached the entrance to Naka's house. "Obachan!" Naka called out. "Obachan, what is that you're cooking? I think even the gods themselves are drooling over that smell. Did you get a pig at the market?"

"I got more than a pig at the market my dear," his Grandma asserted from the kitchen. "You haven't smelled a thing yet."

"Your grandma never disappoints, Naka." Kane rubbed his stomach in anticipation. "Do you think she's going to add that special glaze she makes?"

"She hasn't made it in over two weeks, so I'd say it's possible. It's tough to get all the ingredients necessary, though. The soybeans and grain are easy enough to come by, but garlic and especially ginger are expensive and tricky to find."

"But so worth it when she pulls it all together."

Naka nodded. He and Kane then proceeded to set up for dinner, taking four woven mats and placing them around the table in the main space. When sitting on the mats, the table came up to the bottom of his rib cage, although he was a little shorter than the typical dinner guest. They then got the two cushions they had and placed them where Naka's grandmother and father would be sitting. They then went to the kitchen to grab ti leaves and chopsticks and set them down at each of the four spots.

"Seriously, Obachan, this smells great. What are you cooking?"

"Oh, just the typical shredded pork, but with a little twist this time," she smiled. "I figured we haven't had the soy glaze you like so much in a long time."

"Woo!" Kane exclaimed, punching the air a few times. "That's wonderful news aunty. I've been dreaming about that glaze for weeks ever since I first tried it. How come no one else in the village makes that?"

"Oh," Naka's grandmother smiled. "People here, they like to stick to the Nakai food and the Nakai traditions. It's important to keep those traditions and customs alive—especially when those traditions and customs are suppressed. Eating food is an important part of connecting yourself to where you're from, because once you consume it, it goes to the very heart of you."

Kane and Naka nodded.

"But still," she continued. "It's also important to try pieces of a different culture. Just as our food connects us to our ancestors and ourselves, trying and learning about food from a new culture connects us to the people of that tradition. So, it's important for Naka to eat this food, which helps him connect to part of his story, but it's also important for us to eat it, Kane. And then on a personal level, Naka's mother gave me this recipe, so when we eat it, it also connects us to her."

Naka shifted in his seat. Kane nodded, more solemnly this time. "I think more people should have your outlook, aunty," he noted. "If nothing else, we'd have a lot more delicious food to eat."

For the next while, Kane and Naka helped Naka's grandmother prepare the rest of the food, although she did the heavy lifting. The food had just finished cooking when Naka's father came home.

"Hello, my wonderful family!" he bellowed as he entered the house. "Mom, you have outdone yourself yet again. Several people stopped me on my way here and asked me about that amazing smell wafting from our home." He turned to Kane. "A visitor! Welcome, Kane. I trust you're keeping Naka out of trouble?"

Kane smiled. "Yes sir, for the most part."

"Good, good. Some trouble is healthy for the soul, after all. Naka, how were the rice fields today?"

"Kane and I worked our way through the second rice pond today. The plants are growing in well—even better than this time last year. I think this could be a good year for us."

Kane nodded. "Boto was a real jerk to Naka today though."

Naka looked sharply at Kane. "He tends to do that," Naka's father chimed in. "What happened this time?"

"Well, Naka showed up a little past the sun today, but not too late at all. We had it worked out. But Boto came over and gave him an earful anyway. He started talking about how Naka had the worst of both sides of his heritage."

"Kane, stop. We don't need to talk about this," Naka spurted out.

"He said that?" Naka's father fumed. "Naka, has he talked to you like this before?"

Naka nodded. "He mentions my blood every other time he chastises me. It's not a big deal though—I know he's wrong and I know his views are wrong. It's fine."

"He shouldn't be able to get away with that," said Naka's father. "Things should be different. We shouldn't have to listen to bigots like him." He then hit his fist on the table and switched to the Nakai language in his anger. "We shouldn't have to listen to the commands of these land overseers anyway. We should work the land on our own as it was meant to be. They should be paying us for our yields, not the other way around."

Naka's grandmother piped up. "Now Koa, my son, stop with that talk. You're in a safe place to say such things here, but you don't want these words to become a habit and slip out around others who would view them differently. If an overseer or magistrate were to walk by and hear you shouting in Nakai, you would have far bigger problems than an errant comment from a hateful man. Do not be so reckless. Now, we came together tonight to eat as a family. Let's not tarnish the ono food I made with talk of what's wrong with our society. There are plenty of other opportunities for that discussion."

Naka's father looked down and inhaled deeply. "You're right mom, of course. This time is one for rest and support, not rebellion." He turned to Kane and Naka. "Boys, I'm sorry for yelling. Now, let us sit down to eat obachan's delicious food and thank the gods for the meals they have provided."

He handed Naka's grandmother the serving spoon as a sign of respect for the matriarch of the household. In turn, she scooped up some rice and offered it to Kane as the guest rite. Kane nodded his head in acceptance and thanked her for the meal. Once everyone had been served, they began to eat. The meal was truly delicious. Naka's grandmother had perfected the sweet, savory glaze, which was unlike anything else in the village.

As they finished the last of the food on their ti leaves, Naka's father cleared his throat. "I found some pearls on my dive today, so I bought a little present to surprise you all." He stood up and went to his room to retrieve the gift. "You've all been working very hard, and it's showing in what you've brought to our family." He turned to the two boys. "I especially would like to acknowledge the great work you two have done in the fields in only your second year working. It's already looking like a record-breaking harvest for our families. Now that you're becoming men, I thought it fitting to show you one of the perks of adulthood."

He pulled a clear bottle containing a brown liquid out from behind his back. "Tonight, I thought we could try some okolehao to celebrate our recent successes in the fields, in the reefs, and in the weaving houses. What do you all think?"

Kane's eyes grew wide with excitement. "I think yes! Naka, we should try this!"

Naka paused for a second, and then nodded. "Ok, dad, if you think that we're ready for it."

"I do," replied Naka's father. "Mom, would you like some as well?"

The old woman smiled. "I would, yes. It's been some time since I had okolehao."

Naka's father smiled. Let me get the cups then. He went to the kitchen and brought back four copper mugs, which he reserved for special occasions and important guests. He uncorked the bottle and poured a small amount into two of the cups and slightly more in the other two. He raised the cup in front of him. "To family, and to our success this year. May our hard work always pay off."

"Kanpai," Naka's grandmother said, nodding and holding up her cup. Naka and Kane took her lead and said the word as well. "Kanpai!"

The bitterness of the drink overwhelmed Naka's senses and he coughed as he swallowed the gulp. He felt the liquid burn down his throat and make a home for itself in his stomach. The drink wasn't exactly pleasant, but there was something not altogether unpleasant about how he felt afterwards. He looked at Kane to see if he felt the same and could see the same feeling in Kane's eyes. Despite the pained look on his face, however, Kane turned to Naka and asked "again?"

After the third drink, Naka's father imposed a break on the young men. "I can see you wobbling already, Kane. And Naka, you're looking a bit flushed. A rest will do you well. Here, let me get you some water."

Naka looked to his grandmother. "Obachan, how is it that you don't look affected by this stuff at all?" Naka could feel the warmth of the alcohol on his face and wondered what he looked like.

"Practice, my dear. With practice you will be less affected, but more importantly, you'll be able to hide just how affected you are," she said with a wink. "When you get to be my age, you'll have figured out how to handle pretty much everything that comes at you."

"I feel great," stated Kane. "This stuff is amazing—I could talk to anyone right now. I bet I could even stand talking to Boto."

Naka snorted. "Not me. If anything, this stuff makes me want to punch him even more than I already do."

"And that," said Naka's father, after walking back into the room, "is why you shouldn't drink and then go out in public. At least not until you learn to handle yourself like your grandmother. Now," he continued, "the key to drinking okolehao, or soku, or anything alcoholic, is to drink plenty of water. If you don't drink enough water, you will regret it in the morning—especially when you get to be an old man like me. Of course, judging from your face, Naka, and that goofy grin you're wearing, Kane, all the water in Godsdorf won't totally save you from feeling the effects of tonight tomorrow morning. Now drink up!"

The two downed their cups of water and went to the kitchen for a refill, pouring more water from the containers that the elders of the village made by drying gourds from the various ipu trees around the village. "Man, tonight was great," said Kane. "We got to eat some of that delicious glaze, hear some of your grandmother's stories, and top it all off with our first okolehao. If this is what adulthood is like, I want it right now."

Naka smiled. "I'm glad you're enjoying yourself. I'm still not sure I like the stuff—I feel like I'm not in control of myself right now."

"That feeling is what I like the most!" exclaimed Kane, and the two friends laughed. They drank the rest of their water and went back to the main room to help clean up the dinner.

Later that night, after Kane went home, Naka's father called to him from the living room.

"Naka," he said, "before you go to bed tonight, I want to talk to you for a second."

Naka sensed where this was going. "About Boto?"

"About Boto, and about other, broader things. Boto's comments—not only are they unacceptable, but they're completely wrong on top of that."

"I know that, dad."

"I know you know, but I want to elaborate. Boto comes from a place where he was far removed from the coast, its culture, and its people. He was far removed from the Nakai way."

"Right. I can't imagine he would have been named Boto had he been born anywhere close to our village."

Naka's father laughed. "No, no probably not. Then when he grew up, he went to school—all land overseers go to schools, as you know. These land overseer schools, they teach people some good skills, like math, writing, and other such things. But they also instill in Yamahito folk like Boto a sense that their people deserve to rule over the common folk, and over the common Nakai folk especially. When you combine that with a lack of understanding of our culture, or the gifts of our people, you get a dangerous and inaccurate result. You get prejudice, which by definition is unfounded on rational thought.

"Boto is in a position of influence over people. A position in which he can demand payment from those he oversees beyond what is required of them by law. He has the power to bankrupt many in our village and to take away our livelihoods, and all he has to do is write down a compelling enough excuse."

Naka nodded. "I understand. I shouldn't pick any fights with him or do anything that would give him a reason to punish our family. I know that. But sometimes it just seems that he hates me and wouldn't need any other reason at all."

Naka's father smiled. "Actually, that's not what I was going to tell you. We absolutely should pick fights with Boto and other prejudiced people like him. We just need to do it intelligently. We'll never win by singling out only Boto and his bad ideas. We need to tackle the root of the issue."

"How can we do that?" Naka asked. "What is the root, dad?"

"That," replied Naka's father, "is a long conversation best saved for another time."

Naka groaned. "Come on, really? That's what you used to tell me when I was a kid, but I'm becoming a man now. Or did you have so much okolehao that you already forgot you gave it to me?"

Naka's father laughed. "You'll have the answers to your questions before too long. For now, I just want you to promise me that no matter what, you will always try to look past who people are on the surface and understand where they come from. If you can do that, and perhaps even convince others to do the same along the way, then eventually Boto and people like him will begin to understand others too."

"But what if I can't look past the surface? What if I can't see where someone comes from?"

"You won't always be able to understand someone's origin completely. You won't always be able to shake loose your preconceived notions. Assumptions and stereotypes are part of being human. But, if you always at least try to understand someone's path, and if you take time to acknowledge where your own judgments come from, then you can make the change that will help our people most. And you have something that most people in all of Sokoku do not."

"And what is that?"

"You have your heritage: Nakai on one side, and Yamahito on the other. You have an edge on understanding both cultures, because you belong to both cultures."

Naka shook his head. "That would be nice if it were true, dad. But I don't belong to any culture at all. Boto and his people won't accept me, and this land will never truly be mine as it is yours and obachan's."

Naka's father sighed. "Your heritage may not always feel like a gift. I understand that. But I believe it is, and I believe that one day you will believe it too. Now," he said, patting Naka on the shoulder. "It's getting late. You need your sleep to wear off the okolehao, and it would be best not to raise the ire of Boto again with a second tardy arrival tomorrow."

"Good night, dad. Thank you again for the drink. I love you."

"I love you too, son."

Raban

At the sun's highest point, Muni felt her stomach rumble. Raban was also beginning to feel peckish.

"I've got some thuma leaves," Muni said, as she opened a small bag in her pack full of cold, stringy plant matter.

Raban shook his head. "These leaves are not the food for adventurers. Hold my spear, Muni," Raban said, as he started to take off his pack.

"Give me some of those bitter things. I'm going to climb up to the canopy and see if I can find us something better. I bet this area is unpicked."

Raban rested his hands on the trunk and stuck his lower talons into the bark. His knees shook a little. While his skills in the ancient art of talon climbing were improving, he still felt a bit shaky. He steadied himself with his wings and started to climb. Every step up needed a new careful grip of the bark with his talons. The tree's bark was thick and soft from the rain, so it was easy to stick his curved talons into it. After some climbing, he got to a branch at the canopy level, and Raban steadied himself upon it.

He propped himself up a bit and started to peel back large chunks of the wet bark, revealing the soft furry inner wood of the trunk. This wood was covered in tiny tree ants, but they weren't worth picking because they were too fast and had almost no taste.

After only a few minutes, Raban found what he was looking for! To the untrained eye, it would look like just a small hole, the opening barely big enough for a youngling's finger, but Raban knew better. While he had only seen a hole like this three times before, Raban's dad had trained him.

He wadded up his sister's thuma leaves and chewed them. Once they felt mushy enough, he spit some back onto his finger and wiggled his covered finger into the little hole. The wood around it started to wiggle as if the tree was about to sprout new branches. Raban waited until the squirming approached the hole and pulled his finger out. Two beady eyes on a thin pale head ripped open the hole. Its forked tongue chasing after his thuma covered fingers. Without hesitation. Raban grabbed its tiny ophidian head, and with the flick of his wrist, cracked it. He pulled out its lifeless lanky body. It was one of the longest ones that Raban had ever seen, it was nearly long as him!

"Hey Muni! I hope this will do instead of the thuma leaves," Raban called down with a taunting smile.

She looked up. When she recognized what Raban was holding, her face beamed with excitement. Fresh Slange was her favorite food! It wasn't an accident why his father taught him how to catch it so well.

Raban's stomach started to growl as he thought about the juicy meat that he had in his hands.

"Alright, Muni, I'm coming down." Raban said as he tossed the dead Slange down to Muni. He had expected her to be looking at him as he called down, but she was looking down, pushing the bag of thuma leaves back into her pack. The Slange meat flew right past her, unnoticed, bouncing off the bridge and falling to the groundfloor.

"MUNI!" hollered Raban.

She looked up and then looked down at the groundfloor, realizing what happened.

"Rabe! Why did you do that?" Muni cried.

"How was I supposed to carry the Slange and climb down?"

"I don't know, but why didn't you warn me to catch it!"

She had a fair point. Raban's heart sank a bit. He was excited to eat something other than thuma leaves. He was mostly expecting to find some small beetles in the canopy. It had been years since they had found a wild Slange.

"Well that's our luck. I guess we still have my thuma leaves we can eat," said Muni.

As Raban climbed down from the branch, he shook his head.

"No, Muni, I'm not going to eat those damn thuma leaves, even if I starve! I got us that Slange to eat, and eat it, we will!"

"How do you propose we do that? I don't expect that you will find another Slange, even if we checked a bunch more trees!"

"That might be true, but I don't plan to find another one. Like you said before, we don't use our bird side enough. Let's glide down to the groundfloor and grab it. You know I would go down there by myself and climb up, but my legs are tired, and the trunk's base is always harder to climb"

He glanced down. He could see exactly where the Slange was lying. It was not too far down, and then they could just continue the journey down there on foot. It would take a bit longer to wade through the brush, but they could still make it to Great Auntie's by dark.

Muni glanced back and forth from the groundfloor to Raban.

"I don't know...I feel like we can find some beetles on another tree and eat my thuma leaves and be fine."

"Wait, Muni, are you scared of going down to the groundfloor?"

"No! I feel like you made a mistake and now want to change the whole trip because of it. The groundfloor is muddy and gross. Let's just move on."

"Whoa, I think you might be more than just afraid of getting those talons a little muddy. Have you ever even been on the groundfloor? Or are you still a pure nester?" Raban asked.

"I don't know why that matters…" Muni looked down at her talons.

"Wow, little sister! You are way too old to be a pure nester! It's time you spread those wings and changed that. For the sake of Slange meat, could there be a better reason to go down?"

Muni stared down at the groundfloor and her beak clicked.

"I guess you're right. My stomach won't stop begging anyways." She smiled.

"Like mother always said, 'the stomach is the only friend that will never lie,'" Raban replied with a smile.

"Okay, well then for our stomach friends, let's go. I'll follow your lead."

Raban nodded and opened up his wings. He had only been down to the groundfloor four times in his life. Yet without hesitation, he perched up on the bridge's post. In one move, he swooped down in a long crescent moon shape. He landed with a soft tumble right next to where the Slange landed.

He picked it up and waved it over his head at Muni. She stuck her tongue out and jumped down. Her glide was more graceful than his, and she landed right next to Muni without even a sound.

"Well I guess not all of us are equal parts bird" Muni quipped with a smile. "Now are we going to finally eat this or what?"

Raban smiled too. He ripped it in half with his talons and gave the juicier bottom half to Muni. They both dug right into it with their beaks, crunching the small bones alongside the meat.

The salty insides made his mouth water, but he could not stop from eating more and more. The juices dripped from his beak. It tasted like briny fruit juice.

They passed the water jug between them as they devoured the thin but meaty serpent. After a while of pecking sounds and gulps, there was no longer any sight of the Slange, and their water jug was empty.

"Hey, thanks again for finding that for us," said Muni as she looked back up at the bridge. I think it was worth it even if it meant this little detour."

"Agreed, and it will also work out now for one other reason."
"And what is that?"
"I will give you one guess, but I hope you figure it out…"
"Hm are you hoping to find some berries or more food?"
"Nope…"
"Come on, Rabe, I don't know, just tell me."

41

"Well I think you can figure it out, and here's a heads up this time—catch!" Raban tossed the empty water jug at her. She caught it with her left talon before it hit the ground.

"Oh, right, we need more water," Muni said, scratching her head feathers. "But how am I supposed to find the river from down here? I can't look down to find it?"

"Wow, mother and father did not train you well before they left. I guess that's why they had to train me extra hard. Listen, it's very simple. All you need to do is follow the green reeds, the thicker they are, the closer you are to the water!"

"In that case, let's go check over there." Muni pointed at a pod of reeds hiding behind a split tree in the distance.

"Well I guess sometimes great eyesight can make up for bad training."

"Alright don't be too jealous that I have real bird eyes, Rabe. Let's go check it out!"

Rabe laughed, and Muni skipped ahead towards the crooked tree.

As they approached the tree, Muni stopped, and her wings stiffened. When Raban approached, she had her hands over her mouth, and signaled for him to be silent. There was some rustling from the other side of the tree. Then suddenly, silence. Raban motioned for them to move forward. After reaching the tree, there was a small growl from inside tightly packed reeds.

Raban wondered if it could it be one of those Ursa bears that his father warned about. He had also heard a Huginn Warrior claim that the bears were planning to invade Arbornesta.

Raban approached slowly with his polespear pointed at the center of the reeds. Muni was also staring at the reeds and walked behind him, her staff raised high, ready to pounce at whatever came out.

"It sounds big…. Do you think it's a Spotted Samata?" whispered Muni.

Raban shook his head. Nobody alive had seen one of those ancient cats; they were long gone.

"No, I don't think so, but I think it could be an Ursa bear. I heard they might be sending scouts over the mountains."

Raban stood in the V-shape of the split tree trunks. He aimed his polespear carefully at the rustling and looked back at Muni. She was scared but nodded at him. Like their father always said, defense sometimes needed to be proactive. He took a deep breath, and, at release, he threw the polespear as hard as he could into the reeds.

It flew right in and hit something! Out from the reeds, a Giant River Otter sprung on its hind legs, the polespear sticking out from its back. The otter thrashed around, trying to pull the spear out of its back, but it was lodged deep, right above the base of its tail. As it struggled to pull the spear out, it turned and saw Muni, who was sticking out from the right side of the tree trunks trying to see what was happening. The creature hissed, exposing its sharp fangs and bounded right towards her.

"Muni, watch out!" Raban called.

The beast jumped forward with his claws extended. Its brown hairy body was a blur as it struck into Muni. She blunted the flying body's impact by side stepping away and hitting its body with her staff. The otter tumbled backwards into the brush, and Muni flew back into the mud, right behind Raban. The otter jumped back on its hind legs and hissed again. This time it moved even faster, diving forward with its front fangs aimed right at Muni.

"Give me the staff!"

His sister threw her staff right into Raban's extended hand. He turned back just as the otter flew around the other side of the tree. Without thinking, Raban swung around, and the staff connected with the otter's face. The smack stunned the otter enough to make it fall backwards. The end of polespear hit the ground first, pushing through the otter's abdomen. It ripped through like wet thuma leaves.

"Eeeeeeeeeh!" hissed the otter. Its eyes closed, and it twitched one last time.

Raban let out a heavy sigh. He looked down and his hand were shaking. Muni's staff, their Great Grandmie's, had a clump of otter hair on its end and was stained with blood.

"Rabe! That was amazing! You saved us!"

Muni hugged him from behind.

"Yea that was a close one. For Huginn's sake, I thought they cleared all the wild predators from this part of the forest. I guess not."

"What if you hadn't thrown father's spear! We would have been eaten for sure!"

Raban hadn't acknowledged what Muni said. His head throbbed with thoughts.

"Well at least we've got a nice welcome present for Great Auntie. This should be enough meat for all of us to eat for a few weeks. Also, looks like we will have another water jug soon," Raban said as he tapped the staff on the otter's abdomen.

Now that the excitement had ended, Raban noticed the bubbling sound of water on the other of the reeds. He pushed through them and there he saw it. They had found the Wandering Creek! It would lead them right to the Forest Edge.

"Isn't it going be a pain to drag this giant otter all the way to Great Auntie's?" asked Muni.

"It won't be too bad; we will just need to weave some ropes to drag the body behind us. Do you think you can do something about that? Maybe using some of these reeds?"

Muni smiled, and she went right to work. Her eyes sized up the different reed shapes while her hands felt their thickness.

He grabbed their water jug and headed over to the creek. The creek wasn't as wide as he expected. It looked like he could almost jump across it. The water was running fast and clear; Raban could see large Coki fishes flowing in the current. He dipped his jug into the cold water. He then ran his fingers through it and washed his face. The mountain water felt refreshing.

When he walked back over to the reeds, Muni was nearly complete with two long sets of rope. She motioned to the shoulder loops that she had made. With these straps, they could both drag the otter at the same time.

"Good work! I'm going to keep looking along the creek, see if I can find us anything else useful. Whistle if you need anything."

"Will do!" Muni said. Without looking up from her weaving, she continued to twist the smaller reeds in a pattern around the thicker ones, a pattern their mother taught them.

Raban walked back over to the creek side and start walking along its bank. The babbling of the water almost called for him to dip in, but he kept walking. Some Corvideans loved bathing in water, washing their feathers, splashing around. Raban never cared for it.

Raban's eyes scanned along the bank. He searched for any little crevice and checked each one by sticking his talons deep inside. Behind a little mud pile, he spotted a deep burrow. He carefully reached his long middle talon into the hole and tapped around the inside.

He felt something squishy. He got down and started to dig out the hole, but he felt the squishy animal burrow deeper! His hands chased it down, pushing his wings deeper into this mud hole, and caught it just before it reached too deep. He pulled out his muddy wing, and in his hand, dangling by one leg, a Mudskap! Its long jumping legs were speckled with green spots, but its long body was a deep shade of mud brown, the perfect camouflage for its environment. Its deep sunken eyes darted from Raban to the river. Before Raban could respond, it wiggled out of his hand, and hopped right into the water. Raban chased it to the river bank but hesitated for a second. He hated swimming in cold water, but his curiosity of this rare creature overcame that annoyance. He dove under the water and the coldness overcame his senses. In his plunge, he reached out with his eyes closed towards the river floor. He just happened to catch the left foot of the Mudskap!

44

He stood up, dripping and cold with the Mudskap secured in his hands. He opened a little hole in his hands to look at the creature. It stared so intensely that Raban had to glance away. He remembered that the Huginn monks used to warn about these little creatures. At one Gathering, he heard that these creatures were crafty and possessed by evil spirits. They would try and trick anyone to do their bidding. Yet when he came home and asked his parents, they claimed that these little frogs used to help guide their ancestors on quests, and sometimes even use magical powers to assist them. Nowadays, though, Mudskaps were rarely seen. His parents had never even seen one!

It wriggled in his hand, trying to free itself.

"Let go of me!" it croaked.

"I don't mean to scare you my friend. I've never seen anything like you before... What's your name?"

"Ah, yes, yes, I'm quite certain that you didn't want to scare me. You dug me out and chased after me into a river, just like some other bird that chased after my mother before she had her legs sliced off her and cooked for dinner. Such nice gestures and words you have, stranger."

"Wow! I think you misunderstand. I swear to you that I mean no harm. I'm on a little journey with my sister and was just curious when I first stumbled on your hole."

"Oh yes, right, and now that I think of it, those sound like the last words that one of your strange bird friends told my father before they threw him into a fire and ate him. Probably the same words, right before my grandmother lost her legs, and, gimme a second... oh yes that's right, my grandfather had his little feet nibbled off by you barbarians too. Yes, it's all coming back to me. Well I guess I should follow family tradition, and just give you my legs!" The Mudskap kicked his legs forward, showing him his long feet.

"I'm sorry to hear that. I really don't mean to scare you. I have nothing against your type, and I have enough food for weeks. Can I ask you for your name, friend?"

"Well let me start off by saying that we are not friends! Your type has killed everyone in my family, and you, my supposed friend, just destroyed my family home!"

Raban looked down. The area of the original hole was dug up and unrecognizable. There were new piles of mud everywhere.

"Well I am sorry for damaging your house, and I can help fix that... You must understand I'm not like those other birds. I live in the trees here, and I don't eat land dwelling animals, unless they are killed in self-defense. The Inlanders, the city-dwelling birds are to blame for those horrible killings. Those bird types eat anything and have no qualms killing animals for pleasure or for food. They would even kill me or my sister if they thought it was worth it!"

The Mudskap stopped squirming and started to smile.

"Nice story, meat-eating creature. Your apology can begin by letting me down and letting me go."

"Right, right. I'm sorry. That's fair. I'll let you down."

Raban placed him back down on the mud. For a moment, it looked like the Mudskap might just stay there, but in a flash, it hopped back into the creek and disappeared under the water. Raban didn't chase after him this time.

Raban felt a bit shaken from that experience. He had never thought about Mudskaps like that and had no clue that the Inlanders ate their legs. It disgusted him a bit, how vicious some creatures could be to other creatures.

But before he could contemplate this topic for too long, Raban heard a muffled scream. "Help! Ka'kaw! Ra—"

He turned back to the reeds. He could hear a commotion coming from the other side of them, where Muni was weaving.

Raban ran back over and could hear voices. He began to realize at that moment how foolish he was for not taking his polespear out of the dead otter. All his other weapons were left in his pack, next to Muni. He was defenseless. When he reached the reeds, he slowed down. He peeked through the thick brush and saw Muni standing there, but not alone. There were three soldiers, two of them sitting on top of 5-horned rhinos. One had its bow drawn and aiming right at Muni. His beady eyes staring right at her. The other one on rhinoback was wearing a red shiny helmet and thick red leather wing protectors. On the side of his rhino saddle, there was a marking of a wing and a shovel. He recognized that symbol...They must be Inlanders!

"Go tie n' bag her!" barked the helmeted one.

The other guard, on the ground, pulled out a woven rope and a wooden club and approached Muni.

"What do you want? Stay away! I'll kill you if you come any closer!" Muni cried. She held her staff over her head.

Huginn, what a fighter she is!

The guard stopped and looked back at the helmeted one.

"Put ya bloody staff down, younglin', before I tell my friend, ova' here, to shoot an arruh right thru those tiny lil' wings of yours."

The soldier with the bow regripped his drawn arrow.

Muni didn't flinch. She kept her staff raised high.

On the far side of Muni laid the dead otter and Raban's polespear.

Raban examined the situation. *There is no way I can get over there in time. I need to set a distraction. I only need him to miss once.*

"You ain't givin' me many choices, missy. Put down that bloody staff, now!"

The bowman looked tired from holding the bow taught for this long. It was now or never. Raban sprinted out from the reeds to the left of the rhinobacks. The archer turned and shot his arrow way left. As he notched the next arrow, Raban turned and ran straight towards him, flanking the guard.

Raban jumped feet first and swooped towards him with his wings pulled outward. His sharp talons aimed right at the soldier.

He knocked him off the rhino, and felt his talons dig deep into the guard's chest. He felt the guard's chest bone crack under the pressure.

"Ahh'kaw!" the guard howled.

"Grab my polespear, Muni!" called Raban.

With no questions, she ran over to his polespear. The guard on the ground chased right behind her, but she made it there first. She wiggled the spear free and clashed it against the club of her pursuer.

The helmeted one had turned towards Raban and pulled out his sword. The rhino reared up and began charging his way.

Raban pushed off the wounded guard and ran towards Muni.

However, he underestimated the rhino's speed. When he looked back, the rhino was already almost on top of him. It reared up on its hind legs one more time and kicked Raban right in the head with its massive hoof.

He fell. He could feel the blood trickle down his face feathers, as he fell to the ground. His head was throbbing, and he could not hear anything from his left ear.

He could still see, with one swollen eye, Muni struggle against the other guard. She fought with the strength of a full-grown Arborn and looked like she could beat this guard on her own, but the rhinoback leader charged over to assist his companion. Together, they knocked the spear out of Muni's hands, and tied her up from behind. She wrestled against them the entire time.

"Rabe! I'm sorry!" Muni cried, as she thrashed against their taut ropes.

They threw a bag over her face and knocked her on the head with the club. Her body stopped wrestling. The guard tossed her limp body over the backside of his leader's rhino.

Raban could only think of Muni.

"Ey, finish off that other one and let's go!" barked the commander. The two started to march away with Muni.

Rabe looked up. The bowman was standing above him, dripping blood and holding Muni's staff.

"You little tree-freak! Don't worry, we Inlanders will take great care of your little friend. Lord Chasta is going to enjoy this little present," he wheezed with a snicker.

"If we had more time, I would have my fun with you too, but I guess our time together ends here." He pulled back Muni's staff and with one swoop, cracked down on Raban's bleeding head.

***

Argh...what in Huginn's name happened to me? Raban opened his eyes. He was lying on the ground and his head felt like his heart. He felt around on his head and found a massive bump on the back of his skull.

He touched the top of his forehead. There was a deep gash at his featherline but no blood coming out, which surprised him. He looked down on his body and he had an array of scratches and gashes but none of them were bleeding either. There was not even dried blood on his feathers. The wounds also were not sensitive like he expected. They had a light white foam around the edges and felt cool to the touch. Raban had no explanation for this response. As he sat up, his body felt lighter.

He looked around. There were different tracks of talons and hooves everywhere.

"Muni! Muni!"

He ran in a wide circle, looking for any sign of his sister. He saw two sets of large hoof marks, but no sign of talons after following them for a while. They were on a path towards the Inland. He went back to where he woke up. When he walked near the reeds, he saw a dead otter, next to his polespear and pack.

The sudden memory of what happened came flowing back to Raban. He fell to his knees. The throbbing in his head intensified, and he felt like he was the Giant River Otter with his insides ripped apart.

Why in Huginn's name did they take Muni? What was wrong with those Inland barbarians! Why were they this deep in the forest?

He listened carefully to see if he could hear any sound of hooves or walking, but he could only hear chirping insects. Raban knew that he couldn't chase after them right now and needed to return home and recruit others to help him. He picked up his pack and polespear and turned back towards his home.

Great Auntie is going to have to wait.

Luteo

The Main Square was almost unrecognizable from the night before. Ursa of all shapes and colors filled the stands surrounding the ceremonial stage, and the buzz of excited chatter echoed throughout Berarbor. Nestled at the confluence of the five main branches of Berarbor, the Main Square was often used as a gathering place for a varied mix of community events. The Agronomists took over the square on the equinox of fall to contest which Ursa produced the best pumpkins and apples, and the priests of the Tarsus covered the square in candles and sang tunes of memory during the winter solstice to welcome the coming season. Luteo had fond memories of Kermodei leading the latter ceremony, speaking to the huddled attendees about power and rebirth, his arms gesturing embraces from beneath his layered ritual cloaks.

This day, however, was an entirely different story. The energy in the crowd was one of frenzied excitement. Luteo had witnessed this event each fall as he grew up, seeing each cohort of Ursa make their way from childhood to adulthood, but this time found it entirely unrecognizable from his new vantagepoint. Instead of his usual place on the bleachers surrounding the ceremony, Luteo was standing in a crowd of his closest friends and colleagues from throughout his life. Pern stood next to him, flashing faces through the crowd to his little sister Pruin and generally making light of the entire Liberalia. Luteo turned his head over his shoulder and saw his family sitting behind him. His father's shaggy arm was draped over his mother, comforting her as their eldest and only son left their den. Isabell, on the other hand, looked entirely nonplussed as she likely was too young to truly understand the gravity of the moment. Luteo turned his head back to face the empty stage at the head of the Main Square and re-adjusted his cloak to keep the breeze from chilling his core.

The true magic of the Liberalia was witnessing the arrival of Ursa from the two other kingdens in Godsdorf. The three kingdens were often in varying states of disagreement and disunity, yet year after year managed to settle their differences to celebrate the passage of their young into adulthood. Throughout the year, a traveler or member of another kingden's council might visit Berarbor on occasion, but the Liberalia was the only event where the three kingdens came together in both body and mind. Traveling with each envoy would be the kingden's Denmaster, who occupied the highest seat in each kingden's council. Immediately following the ceremony, the three Denmasters and their respective entourages would convene in the Berarbor Denmaster chambers and negotiate the coming year's challenges and desires. These sessions often ended in curses and heightened voices but offered the only outlet for formal diplomacy.

The excited buzz of voices surrounding Luteo died down to a hushed whisper. Luteo snapped out of his daydream and again faced forward. Denmaster Bern strode out from the darkness on the far side of the square into the sunlight, shaking his paws to the audience surrounding the square, and made his way to the stage flanked by his other Berarbor council members. He paused as he ascended the stage, shaking his hands in a theatrical show of thanks to the audience. Luteo grumbled under his breath as Bern milked the moment for an excessive amount of time; moments like these made it clear Bern was a politician first and a leader second.

As Denmaster Bern took his place on the stage, Kermodei emerged from the same doorway from which Bern's entourage had appeared moments earlier and followed the pathway to the stage wrapped in his ceremonial robes that appeared annually each Liberalia. Despite being the head of the Tarsus Priesthood, and thus seen as an equal figure to Denmaster Bern in the Berarbor government, Kermodei simply ascended the stage and found his seat next to the other Berarbor council members. The council member seated next to Kermodei leaned in the opposite direction, as if Kermodei had a foul odor he was trying to escape.

"Welcome, Denfolk, to the Liberalia!" Bern exclaimed with arms wide and claws extended. His deep voice reverberated on the opposing walls of the Main Square and filled the space with sound. The murmuring of voices surrounding Luteo slowly rose and quickly subsided. "Thank you for joining us in our sendoff of our youth into adulthood – where we say goodbye to our children and hello to our brothers and sisters. This day is forever seared into our minds for good reason. Each Ursa among you has entered the gauntlet of the Liberalia and exchanged parts of their being. No Ursa has survived the Liberalia and returned entirely the same as when they entered." Bern turned his gaze from the crowd surrounding the square and focused on the group of young Ursa standing alone in the center. His eyes passed over Luteo and continued without recognition.

"Each one of you will transform in the coming days. Some things you lose will be painful, and some things you gain will give your life more meaning than it ever had before. But each of you who return will become a thread in the fabric of our society, a star in our night sky." Bern's voice trailed off as he seemed to be overcome with memories. A council member behind him cleared their throat, and Bern snapped back to the moment.

"With that, I would like to begin the ceremony by welcoming our brothers and sisters from our neighboring kingdens. Please, all rise as we introduce our family from Ursolympa and Terrarctos."

The murmuring rose again and Ursa stood and craned their necks to catch a glimpse of the foreign Ursa who so rarely visited Berarbor. Luteo saw some movement from the dark archway to the left of the stage and watched the doorway with intense focus. The square was filled with a strange sound as four armored Ursa entered playing odd bowed instruments that were hoisted on their shoulders. Their armor was covered in dark swirls and shapes that Luteo had never seen before and their large paws strummed the strings stretched taut on the bow frame.

Following the four Ursa into the Main Square, the Denmaster from Ursolympa strode confidently into the light flanked by two other councilmembers. A rotund and scholarly looking creature, the Denmaster had round spectacles and was ornamented with dark streaks in his grey fur. He turned to face the stage holding Denmaster Bern and Kermodei and bowed deeply. The Ursa who initially led him into the square played a final chord which faded into silence, and then turned on their heels in formation to face the stage.

"Thank you, Denmaster Bern, for the warm welcome. For those of you who do not know me, my name is Denmaster Kira and I bring regards from my people, the Olympa, to you and your kind. We have been traveling from the far mountain reaches for the last few days and are grateful to finally be quartered with our rarely-seen brethren. I am accompanied by 16 of our young who will be taking part in the Liberalia." Denmaster Kira swept his short arm back to the door and welcomed the young Olympa from the shadows behind the stage.

The Olympa entered the square in a perfect line, walking in step with each other. They were shorter than most of the Arbora, and Luteo was surprised to notice their fur was generally much lighter, full of greys and whites. *They must have adapted to mountain life*, Luteo thought to himself as he noted their diminutive stature and thick legs. They each carried a pack and wooden walking stick and made their way into the center of the square. As each Olympa passed by Denmaster Bern and the stage, they quickly turned and bowed deeply before continuing. Soon the Olympa were standing in a square of four by four next to Luteo and the Arbora Ursa. Denmaster Kira waited until the last Olympa was in position before making his way onto the stage with his entourage and taking a seat.

The square was once again quiet, as everyone waited patiently for the third and final group to enter. A burst of flame shot out of the dark archway behind the stage, startling everyone in the stands. Luteo almost tripped in shock, as two twirling Ursa somersaulted through the air into the square in a flash of color. The acrobats landed lightly on their feet and again spit fire from a small pipe device that they put to their jaws, bathing the square in red. Scattered applause rose from the audience, as the acrobats tumbled backwards and landed in a lithe stance on either side of the archway. A broad and tall Ursa walked with care into the square, decorated with a maroon cloak and broad sword mounted on his back. His stark bone-white fur stood out strongly from the dimly lit background, and dark circles surrounding his eyes gave depth and gravity to his stare. He surveyed the audience as he paced towards the stage with no apparent rush. Luteo noticed he had been holding his breath and reminded himself to breathe normally. The large Ursa stopped right next to the stage and bowed deeply to the two Denmasters.

"I am Denmaster Arcus of the Terrera. We have walked for many days from the lowland reaches of Terrarctos and bring 12 of our kind to participate in the Liberalia." Arcus' voice was slow and thick like syrup, stretching out vowels in a relaxed drawl. "Terrera, enter." Arcus commanded in a shout, startling many Ursa in the crowd.

Before his last syllable left his mouth, a line of young Ursa burst into the square adorned with bronze armor and carrying ornamented spears. Luteo noticed that the Terrera were taller and more muscular than either the Olympa or the Arbora, with fur that matched the dry browns and greens of the grasslands. The front of the line was led by the tallest and largest, who bore a strikingly similar resemblance to Denmaster Arcus. His eyes were circled in the same dark ring as those of Denmaster Arcus, and his fur was a similar shade of white. As each Terrera passed the stage into the center of the square, they issued a guttural grunt and beat their chest with the paws holding their spears. Luteo watched as Denmaster Arcus' gaze followed the leader of the line, with a face that was both proud and severe at the same time.

The Terrera fell into place and stood at attention next to the Arbora on the opposite side from the Olympa in the center of the square. Denmaster Arcus looked on with approval at the standing Ursa, and then ascended the stage. The two seated Denmasters rose to join Arcus, and all three greeted each other with deep bows. The three Ursa then turned to the audience and walked to the front of the stage, each Denmaster standing in front of their litter of young that were participating in this year's Liberalia. Kermodei and the council members from each kingden quickly filed off the stage and walked towards Denmaster Bern's chambers to prepare for the talks which always followed the Liberalia. The three Denmasters stood alone on the stage.

"To formally finish the welcome ceremony, let us invite our Maiden of the Spring to the stage who will lay the ceremonial wreath." Denmaster Bern's voice echoed through the square. Luteo's eyes trained on the archway behind the stage. From the darkness stepped a small Ursa in a traditional gown carrying a wreath that dwarfed her head and shoulders. As she walked to the center of the square, Luteo felt that he recognized her gait. She turned to place the wreath on a pedestal in the center, and her head emerged from behind the colorful bouquet. Luteo immediately recognized his sister.

Isabell stood happily behind the flowers she had just placed on the podium, and her eyes searched among the young Ursa for Luteo. When her gaze fell on his, she flashed a wide grin and turned back to the stage. Luteo couldn't believe that both his parents and Isabell had managed to keep this a secret from him – participating as the Maiden of Spring was a great honor reserved for the family of a participant in the Liberalia. He turned back to look at his parents and saw his mother wiping tears from her eyes. His father was standing tall and proud, as he watched Luteo and Isabell both playing their parts. Luteo hadn't noticed Isabell had left the ceremony during the entrance of the other Ursa.

Isabell ascended the stage and stood right in front of Denmaster Bern, who immediately placed his hands on her shoulders. Luteo locked eyes with his sister—she looked especially joyous and beautiful in her Maiden outfit.

"What a wonderful sight! Thank you, Maiden of the Spring, and thank you everyone for—" Bern started speaking but Luteo was distracted by a flash of light coming from the darkness behind the stage. Luteo arched his neck to look past the stage but couldn't see anything in the darkness. He scanned the darkness for a few more moments and was about to turn his attention back to the ceremony when another flash gleamed from the darkness. Luteo looked over at Pern, but his friend was still transfixed by the closing comments of Denmaster Bern.

Luteo trained his eyes forward just in time to see a dark shape burst from the archway behind the stage. The proportions of the shape looked wrong to Luteo, as if it had elongated legs and wide flat arms, almost like wings. The audience behind Luteo was starting to notice the disruption, and some Ursa were standing and pointing at the approaching form. Denmaster Arcus turned to face the archway and assumed a battle position with his planted legs. Denmaster Bern wheeled around to face the shape, pulling Isabell around with him.

Luteo pushed his way forward through the other Arbora, trying to get closer to Isabell. The shape continued careening towards the stage and was approaching far quicker than Luteo. Luteo felt as if he were in a nightmare where his limbs moved sluggishly as if through water. He could see the bizarre creature in slow motion, as it spread its wings open to release a shower of small orbs hurling towards the stage. Luteo ran even harder towards the stage, bounding closer to his sister. Denmaster Arcus dove towards the other two Denmasters, tackling them over the stage towards Luteo's advance and away from the incoming figure. Isabell was left standing alone on the stage, her feet frozen.

"Isabell!" screamed Luteo. "Run!"

A flash of light blinded Luteo, and an explosion threw him backwards. The silhouette of Isabell was seared on his retinas, as the stage was bathed in fire. Luteo landed on his back, looking straight up at the branches in the canopy of Berarbor. A high-pitched whining was all he could hear, and the world slid out of his view as he fell into the black.

Naka

Naka woke with a dull, lingering pain in his head and immediately went to the kitchen to
drink more water. He looked out the window and, with relief, saw that the sun was not yet peeking above the horizon. His father and grandmother were, as usual, already gone. He fixed himself some leftover food from dinner and set out to Kane's house.

When he got to Kane's house, he again knocked at the entrance to the home without receiving a reply. *Strange,* Naka thought. *I'm early today. Kane should still be here, unless he left extra early.* He called out and announced his presence and received a groan from inside in response. Naka peeked into the room that let out the voice and laughed.

"Kane," he said, looking at his friend lying in his bed writhing away from the sun. "C'mon, get up. We gotta get to the field before Boto today or he'll add to our tariff."

Kane let out another groan. "I feel like death. Please leave me here alone so Makakua can take me to the underworld."

"I'll get you some water. That'll help. But you're coming to the fields with me. If you need to, once Boto goes to check on the other fields you can relax for a while and I can work the fields, but you gotta at least show your face."

"I can barely stand listening to you right now, let alone Boto. He can go straight to the underworld too. I'll take him with me. Solve two problems at once."

Naka laughed. "I'll give you until the sky warms up a bit, but after that we're gone, yeah?"

"Fine."

Kane got up a few minutes later, rubbing his head and drinking the water Naka brought to his room. "Thanks for this. Man, I feel terrible. Maybe adulthood isn't so great, eh? Come on, I've held us up here long enough."

The fields were just as they left them yesterday, with a few more birds here and there. Having finished weeding the second pond in their rotation, Naka and Kane moved on to the third. Their families together had ten total rice ponds to look after this year, with two others that had their scheduled break from harvesting for the season. The work went normally that morning, and even Boto's daily visit did not make for extra headaches. Naka gave Kane a break in the middle of the afternoon to rest a little and drink more water.

Naka was hard at work on a particularly stubborn weed when Kane cursed. "What in the name of Akuanui…"

Naka shook his head, still working on the weed's root. "Your head still hurts that bad? I'm gonna need some help later, you know. Whether your head hurts or—"

"—No," Kane interjected. "Naka, look around!"

Naka raised his head, about to reply, when he realized that the whole rice pond was bathed in a dim, but penetrating, red light. He looked up, squinting his eyes at the sun, which shone like a crimson lantern. Even during the deepest sunrise or sunset, he had never seen the sun that strong in color.

"What—why is it so red?" Naka babbled. "It's only just past midday; what's going on?"

"I have absolutely no idea," replied Kane. "I've never seen anything like it before."

Naka looked around and realized that he heard none of the noises that normally peppered each moment of a day in the fields. No chirping of the birds, no splashes from the koi in the pond, not even a whistle from the wind. He could see other farmers staring from their own fields a few dozen yards away, each looking on with some mixture of captivation and concern. It seemed no one knew what to do except stop in their tracks and take note of what they saw. Despite the strength of the light from the red sun, Naka noted that it didn't hurt to look into it as it would normally. Still, he thought it best to look away frequently.

The sun blared out the deep red color for several minutes, which in the silence of the moment felt like hours. The sun slowly turned from red back to its typical early afternoon hue and looking at it hurt increasingly until it felt like any other sun. Naka and Kane stood for a moment and tried to process what had just occurred. They looked at each other and took a breath to speak but didn't know what to say.

Naka and Kane looked around at the other farmers and saw that although some of them went back to work, many were leaving the fields for the day and heading back toward the village.

"Are they calling it an early day?" Kane asked.

"Looks like it. Maybe they're going to the village to see if anyone knows what just happened."

Naka looked at their own rice ponds and did some quick math. They had gotten some good work in today but weren't quite done with what they had planned to complete. If they put in extra time in the next few days, though, they could still catch up by the end of the week even if they called it an early day today.

"Should we head to the village too?" Naka asked. "We made some okay progress today and I'd like to see if anyone has any clue about that red sun."

Kane nodded. "Not like I was helping much today anyway, although I actually feel better now."

The two walked back to the village, chatting about why the sun might have turned red along the way. Was it a sign from Akuanui? Did Mahana, the sun god, forget what time of day it was, or get in a fight with his sister Mahina, the goddess of the moon? Or, maybe the red sun meant nothing at all. But how could something that crazy mean nothing? Naka hoped the elders of the village had better ideas than he did.

As they neared the center of the village they began to hear the noise of a large crowd. A man that Naka knew from around town ran up to the two of them in a frenzy.

"Naka! It's your father! He's raised a mob. Come!"

Naka and Kane looked at each other with matching concerned glances and then hurried to the center of the village. When they passed the last house blocking their view of the center, a huge crowd came into view. There looked to be about two hundred people. Naka had only ever seen this many people in one place at the New Year celebrations. The crowd buzzed with an agitated energy and Naka could see people shouting at each other in confusion. At the center of the huddle was Naka's father, shouting over them. Naka could see Kane's parents to his father's left, and some of the village elders to his right. Naka's father waited for the noise to die down a little and then spoke.

"Nakai of the village of Manaolana! Listen to me! This sun is the sign we have been waiting for!" As he spoke, the crowd fell quiet, listening to his words. Naka was surprised. His father had always been popular and well-liked in the community, but he kept to himself and did not typically lead or direct others. When people needed guidance, they had the elders as primary options. He'd never seen his dad act like this before. He spoke with a fire and a passion in his voice that were impossible to ignore.

"How long have we waited patiently under Yamahito rule? The great conquering occurred even before our grandparents' grandparents were born, and what has happened since? The Yamahito have moved onto our lands. They have tried to replace our gods with their mountain spirits. They have tried to take our language and our very culture. But they have not succeeded. We worship the gods in private and draw our strength from their guidance. We speak our language behind Yamahito backs and whisper our most treasured secrets."

Naka cursed under his breath. *What is he doing?* Naka shook his head. *Dad knows that worship of the gods and speaking in the Nakai language are against the law. With a crowd this large, it's a certainty that his words will get back to Boto and the other overseers in charge of this village. They'll bring him before the magistrates at once and throw him in prison for his heresy. What on earth is he thinking?*

Naka's father continued. "We keep our culture strong, but our ways and traditions cannot survive for much longer. A shark cannot survive in a fishnet. These laws were made to contain our culture, to weaken it, and then to break it. Instead, we must break free of these rules placed on us. If we fight back, we can win. If we do not, our culture will die. It will die so slowly and subtly that our grandchildren, or our grandchildren's children, will not even notice when they have lost touch with our ways of life forever."

The crowd buzzed with excitement, and Naka saw some heads nodding in the crowd. Still, many looked just as unsure as Naka felt. *It will take more to convince the others,* he thought. Then, Kane's father stepped forward. "He's right," Kane's father added. "What we propose may seem like madness to you, or even suicide. But it is not so—not if we work together as we have always worked together. The Yamahito have better weapons, yes, but they are a more fractured society, rife with elites at each other's throats in their grabs for power. We can come together as a united people, because we share a culture that has been oppressed from all sides. Just as we feel this subjugation of our culture right here in our village, so too do the Nakai in Kalani and in the other coastal cities."

"How do you know that other Nakai will join with us?" Asked a voice in the crowd. "What if they do nothing to come to our aid?"

"They will help," said Naka's father. "I know they will help, because we have been in contact with some of them for some time."

Several gasps rose above the crowd, including Naka's. *How did dad contact Nakai in other cities without me knowing? How long has that been going on?*

"Unfortunately, we cannot share more details without jeopardizing our movements," Naka's father continued, gesturing to the crowd, "especially in as open an environment as this. Those of us standing in front of you today realize, of course, what our actions will mean for ourselves and our families." At these words Naka stood taller, hoping to meet his father's eyes. His father could not see him through the crowd. "Those of us up here speaking today know what we risk for ourselves should no one else wish to join with us in this cause. But we also know what our community risks if no one stands up at all."

Kane's father added, "for now, everyone, head home and think about what we've proposed here. We need to be unified as a people for this to work, and to unify we must weigh our different perspectives and come to a conclusion as a community. That is our way. Let us meet again this evening to make that decision."

As the crowd left, Naka hurried out of the village center without saying goodbye to Kane. He had many questions for his father, but he felt clouded in his judgment and needed time to process what he had witnessed.

Naka got home before anyone else. He sat out back behind his home and whittled as he sometimes did when trying to puzzle something out. The knife handle he was working on was just beginning to take shape when his grandmother came out from around the corner of the house. She walked to him and waited a few feet away from where he sat. He looked up at her and nodded at her. She took the invitation and sat with him, not saying anything.

After a time, Naka spoke. "Obachan, what was dad thinking?" Naka could feel his voice raising but couldn't control it. "The overseers will have him thrown in prison for those words. If he's lucky, he'll only be whipped raw. More likely they will kill him for that plan of his." He paused, as the full weight of the situation hit him. "They'll take our fields. Even if he lives, they'll take our fields and we won't be able to support ourselves without the yearly harvest. And Kane's parents! The overseers will take away their family's right to the fields as well. He may have ruined both our families! What of our future?"

"Naka," his grandmother started in a calm tone. "Your father did what he did precisely because he *is* thinking of our family's future. He's thinking of you, and of me, and of Kane's family as well. He's thinking of our village, and beyond that, he's thinking of the Nakai people and our way of life. Your father knows the risks. Kane's parents know the risks as well and support your father. They were by his side in the crowd, after all. Kane's parents have had as much a hand in this plan as your father."

"But this plan of his, how can it possibly succeed? Does he forget that the Nakai lost to the Yamahito centuries ago in the conquering? Since then, the Yamahito have only grown stronger and better at their ironworking. What weapons do we have that can match theirs? The shared bond of Nakai brothers and sisters? How can such an intangible strength match the cut of a steel sword?"

Naka's grandmother chuckled. "You ask good, big questions as usual, Naka. Cherish that ability. I would prefer your father get into the specifics of his plan with you himself, but I will tell you that your father shares your affinity for questions. He has asked these questions of himself—and, privately, of others—for many years. He now believes he has the right answers to those questions, and knowing what I know of his plans, I can tell you that I believe too. Your father is not known for irrational thinking or enraged outbursts. You have known him for your entire life; you know his reserved and thoughtful nature. Do not mistake the passion you saw in the crowd today for reckless abandon."

Naka nodded. "I still have many questions," he said.

"Questions that your father will want to answer when he returns home. He should arrive before too long. Now, help me prepare dinner and do not fret about the big picture for the moment."

Raban

Brrrring... brrring... brrring.
The Gathering bells called like the birds amongst the trees, and the monks scattered around to form a wide circle. Other Arborns gathered around the circle. All of them humming together and rocking their bodies in rhythm. In the center of their circle, stood a cloaked figure, holding a bright torch next to a small wooden altar with a large veiled object sitting on it. On the final bell toll, the figure placed the torch on the hidden object, and it slowly caught on fire. The smoke from the burning rose above them and the surrounding crowd. Now shrouded in a thick cloud of rising smoke, the cloaked figure began to chant:

The smoke rises this morning with the sun;
To greet our faces, our feathers, and our wings,

The smoke flies above us with the sun;
To sustain our bodies, our trees, and our world.

In the trees, we live and pay homage to Huginn,
In the nests, we sing and offer bondage to Huginn.

And together, we state the truth and embrace
our Heritage
our Future,
and our Faith.
Now say with me the words our Great Leader wrote for us.

The monks and the entire crowd joined in unison:

I believe in one King Raven, the Father all-powerful,
maker of this land and this sky, all that is seen and unseen.

By the power of His spirit, He forged with humankind and created new life.
Through Him, all of us were made. We were made in His image and brought to earth for
His mission.

Yet, we were not ready. We believed the lies of the human, the dreadful lifestyle of the
humans.
We didn't follow His Good Word. We betrayed our Father.

61

For our sake, He sacrificed Himself. He suffered, died, and was buried.
On the third day, He rose again and ascended into the sky.
He will come again in glory and splendor to judge the living and the dead.
His Kingdom will have no end.

We look forward to continuing His spirit here on earth, for righting our wrongs,
and we look for the future judgement of our one and only King Raven.

The crowd paused and raised their wings together.

As the smoke rises, We shall also rise.
As the smoke flies, We shall also fly.
Ka'kaw!

One of the monks in the circle stepped forward and walked to the front of the altar. "Today, we have Greatness incarnate in our midst," he said. "Our Gathering is not being led today by just any monk, but instead the Great Leader, himself. The Great Great Grandson of Huginn, the Uncontested, the All-Father of Arborns, and the one ruler of us all… Vali!"

The cloaked figure stepped out from behind the altar and the wall of smoke. Silence swept over the crowd. He was taller than he looked from behind the altar. He pulled his cloak down to reveal his face and smiled. The smile cracked across his egg-white face and he stared at the crowd with steadfastness. His eyes looked heavy, like they were dragging his entire face down, but they were soft and green like a much younger Arborn. He smiled wider and his teeth shone sharp and bright like his eyes.

He cleared his throat with a cough and began. "Thank you all for coming to the Gathering, this beautiful morning. As you all know, our year comes to a close soon, and it is important that we Gather every day together to celebrate it. We have so much to be thankful for this year."

There was a strong murmur of agreement from the crowd.

"The Good Words of my ancestor, Huginn, are being spread as we speak in the cities of the Inlanders. Under my direct orders, I have dispatched many monks into the cities of these heretics to try and convert them to the Right Way of Life. Let us send our warmest prayers to these Monks. They have risked everything for the cause. Some have been caught and tortured. Some have even died! But their lives and their missions were not in vain! I am pleased to announce that we have recruited over five dozen new families to our community this year alone!"

The crowd broke out in a loud applause and one rowdy monk in the back began to chant chanted "Ka-kaw Vali! Ka-kaw Vali!"

Vali raised his large wings and it grew quiet.

"We have also, under my direct orders, sent multiple raids on Inlander's farms that are approaching the Forest Edge. Our message has been clear. If you dare live the human way, if you dare disregard your rightful King Raven heritage, if you dare reject the Truth for the easy way of life, if you dare move too close to us without paying respect, we shall strike! We shall not send weak warnings with our tongues, but we shall cut with our talons. With the full fury of our King Raven blood, we shall strike these human-worshipping inbreds from the entire land of Godsdorf!"

After this proclamation, the crowd erupted! The circle of monks locked wings to prevent the masses from surging too close to Vali. There was electricity in the air. Vali stepped back to the altar, giving time for the crowd to revel in their excitement. When he returned to the center, he raised his wings and the crowd silenced again, this time a bit more slowly.

"We have come so far! The vision of my ancestor, and our Great Leader, Huginn, was right when he proclaimed us to be Birds first, and humans, second. Our lives back in the trees, where we belong, has brought so much more—"

There was commotion in the crowd, as one Arborn, pushed their way to the front.

"Let me through! Let him hear me, please! I have something everyone needs to hear," called the shoving Arborn. Several monks grabbed this intruder, hitting him on the head, and pulling him away from the circle, but Vali called to them.

"My children, please let this member speak, he sounds frightened."
Without raising his head, the intruder bowed to Vali.

"Thank you, dear leader, … I have just returned from a journey, and yes, my voice may sound frightened because I am. My name is Raban Mellori. Son of Rehassa and Urt Mellori. My sister, and I went to visit my Great Auntie Kit at the Forest Edge, but we were brutally attacked by Inlander guards! My sister, Muni, was kidnapped by these guards. I don't know why, but they were deep in our forests, much further in than the Forest Edge. I tried my best to fight them, but they were on rhinoback and outnumbered us… I still have their blood on my polespear."

Raban raised his weapon over his head, which still had dried blood on the end, from his earlier fight. This dramatic action had its desired effect. The crowd wanted more blood.

"If this boy was brave enough to fight, I am too!" cried one Huginn monk, who had hit Raban in the head when he first arrived.

"Huginn-damned barbarians in our forests, we need to kill them all!" cried another.

"Damned Melloris, always finding trouble, but I will not stand for this!"

"A little Arborn girl with Inlanders, I've had enough of this depravity!"

More comments like these sprang up throughout the crowd. The electricity was recharging.

Raban continued with his head tilted down.

"I beg you Great Leader, Vali. Please send our finest warriors and our passionate people with me and help me lead an attack against the city of Chasteria, where my little sister is being held. I'm ready, I just need help."

The crowd agreed and started chanting "Ka-kaw!" as they had before.

Vali nodded along and raised his wing tips high.

"My dear son, Raban. Thank you for coming to me. I cry inside for the loss of my Daughter and your sister, Muni. This sick invasion of our land and our people will not be tolerated by the Inlanders. I'm also happy to hear that you tried to fight them off. You are a true Arborn, and a true Mellori! Your family's bravery is well-noted, and this act of personal boldness does not surprise me. I would love to send you on a mission of vengeance for your sister, but I'm afraid I must first ask—because you still look young—have you undergone your Ceremony yet?"

Raban shook his head. "No, Great Leader, I have not."

Vali's heavy eyes glanced down. "Well, when are they planned? You must know that no one without completing the Anting ritual can fight in the name of our community, the Good Book says so. I cannot let you lead an attack without this preparation."

Raban knelt now. His frustration was boiling over. He thought this could be an issue. All he could think about was Muni's face before those Inland guards put their bag over it. He started to cry.

"Great leader, you don't understand. My sister is the last of my kin with me. My parents have left for their own journey and I do not know if they will return. She is all that I have left, and I have pledged to protect her. Please give me permission to go."

The crowd seemed to agree. Many around Raban were tearing up too and nodding along.

"Well, my son, I cannot uproot the foundations that my ancestor has laid, but I can offer you the opportunity to do your Anting ritual as soon as you want."

"Thank you, my Great Leader, for your generous offer. I would like to do it as soon as possible!"

"My son, the fire of Huginn ignites you. I can see that. If you want to drink some Ceremony nectar later tonight, the strengthening effects on your skin will come through in a mere three days, and you will be ready for the rite of Anting then."

Raban's heart surged with impatience. "But I do not want to wait three days, I ask that I do it right now!"

"My dear son, that is brave of you, but without the Ceremony nectar, you skin will be weak and too penetrable for the ants. I fear that your courage will not be enough to survive."

"Please, Vali, my skin, like my sister, cannot wait. I only can imagine what those guards and Lord Chasta are doing to her as we speak."

"Please All-Father, Vali, let this poor boy help his sister!" cried a random bystander.

On Raban's shoulders, he felt tenderness and familiar fingers. He looked up and saw Navine looking down at him with tears in her eyes.

"I'm so sorry, Rabe" she said and hugged him on the ground.

"Navey!" he started to cry harder. Her face brought a sense of warmth throughout his body.

After their embrace, Navine stood back up.

"Please Great Leader, my name is Navine Keen. I'm a close friend of Raban. He has been my friend for many years, and I know his sister Muni very well. I beg that you let him do this Anting Rite and furthermore, I ask that I may do it with him in solidarity. I failed my last Anting rite, and I brought myself and my clan dishonor. I hope to support my friend's courage and redeem myself at the same time. And as the Good Book writes, Friendship Overcomes All. I know we will both be able to overcome the odds together. What says you great leader?"

Raban looked up at Navine in disbelief. He didn't mind putting himself in danger for Muni, but he did not want Navine involved. He looked up at her determined face.

"Wait, what—"

Navine turned and hushed him down. She then pulled him next to her so that they were standing together, in solidarity looking towards Vali.

Vali looked around the crowd. There was a charged silence amongst the Arborns. He paused for a bit and then with some hesitation said.

"The spirit of the King Raven flows in this boy, I cannot deny this fact. I'm also moved by his little friend, here. Due to these unforeseen circumstances, I shall allow this unorthodox rite to occur. I wish you two the best of luck and that the spirit of the King Raven and Huginn are with you."

Turning to the monk circle, he cried, "Prepare the Anting rite!" At this, the crowd threw their wings up in delirious delight and began to chant "Raban!" While those around Raban and Navine, pushed them up onto their shoulders to carry them.

"Well, what in Huginn's name are you up to?" Raban called to Navine, over the cheering crowd.

"You promised that we were going to do the Anting rite, right?" she said with a wry smile.

Raban shook his head and looked skeptically at his friend.

"Well, we are both in this now...and for Huginn's sake, I hope it goes better than your first try."

Navine laughed a bit louder than Raban expected at that.

They started to jostle over the sea of people towards the Anting Tree.

Once they reached the Holy Tree, the crowd stopped and waited. After a while, Vali entered the space with the monks in new robes. They had changed from their brown Gathering robes to the clean white ones of the Ceremony. They gave one to Raban and Navine as well. They put it on over their heads and stood next to Vali.

"We are about to witness the unprecedented, and what I hope is the beginning of a new life for these younglings. Inside of this decaying tree, these two younglings shall enter, and out from this tree, two full-grown Arborns shall return. In honor of our First Father and his wisdom, we all must go through this same purification. It unites us and reminds us of our heritage. Are the two of you ready?"

Raban's voiced escaped him. His throat seemed on fire again. He could only nod. Navine bobbed her head in agreement.

"Well lower them into the tree, we shall begin then!"

Several of the monks proceeded to lift both Navine and Raban up the side of the decaying tree. When Raban and Navine reached the top of the stump, they looked down into its hollow core. Its insides appeared to be empty, with no sign of ants or any life. The inside wood fibers were flaky and peeling off. There was a small ledge about two body lengths down into the core where they could stand.

"Well here we go...we can do this, just remember that this is for Muni!" Navine said with a fleeting smile. She lowered herself into the tree, kicking up some of the dry wood as she fell down to the thin platform deep inside. Raban followed her. They both stood face-to-face on the platform, barely enough space for their wings.

"Not so bad so far" Raban said.

"You've always been such a great friend, Rabe. I don't know what I would do without you." Navine replied. She closed her eyes. Her face radiated in this dark space.

"We will succeed together, Navey, I know it." He was overpowered by how beautiful she looked in this moment.

"You're right, Rabe, I know this won't be in vain."

Raban looked around. "What should I expect?"

"I will tell you the secret of The Anting ritual, Rabe," Navine said with her eyes closed. She paused and took a deep breathe.

"Ants are involved," she said with a big smile.

Raban couldn't help but laugh. His heart leapt to his throat. She always knew how to make him smile.

The monks' chants began to echo inside the trunk.

Every few words, they would hit the outside of the tree, and knock down some flakes and dust inside.

After around the fifth knock, Raban saw some of the first ants. They started to trickle out of invisible holes in the tree's heartwood. They were larger than normal ants and faster. He couldn't see where they were going at first, but then, his talons began to itch. The fire ants were crawling up his legs.

At first, they reached his body and kept crawling up. His entire body felt itchy.

"Don't scratch, Rabe." He looked at Navine. She did not look like her normal self. She looked scared with her wings tightly folded.

"The longer, you can hold out, the better. For both our sakes."

After she said that, Raban couldn't stop thinking about scratching. His skin felt like it was dancing with the ants, screaming for him to scratch a few of them off.

Raban thought that if he could just flick a few of them off, the small relief would be enough. Carefully, with his left hand, he swiped a few ants from his body. He paused. Nothing happened. So Raban flicked a few more off, then started to use both hands to sweep the ants off his body.

Underneath his right palm, he accidentally crushed some of the ants. Navine opened her eyes.

"Oh Rabe, well get ready..."

It felt like the moment before a thunderstorm. The ants broke out in a frenzy. All the ones on his body bit into his flesh at once. They cut right through his skin, like thin thuma leaves.

"HUGINN! MY SKIN!" cried Raban. Navine moved swiftly. She stepped towards him and hugged him as close as she could, pushing most of the ants off his body and onto hers in the process.

"Stop! They are going onto you! What are you doing, Navey!" Raban said as he struggled against her tight hug.

"Rabe, don't forget me."

"No, Navey! Stop this!"

She covered his body in her wings and squeezed even harder. He struggled to get free but failed to get out of Navine's tight grip. He could see blood come through her white robes.

There were still ants biting on his back and his legs. He felt light-headed and nauseous. The insides of the tree began to spin. He closed his eyes, and everything went dark.

Luteo

Luteo stood at the edge of the world and looked out into the abyss below and above. The whole insignificance of it all was a joke—a joke of cosmic proportions. He heard his father's voice from behind him, whispering too quietly for him to understand. He heard his mother singing soft songs from many years ago, the lullabies she sang to lull him into sleep. He heard Isabell's excited giggles, and he remembered fire and light and sound.

He jumped into the void.

***

Luteo awoke with a start. He was lying in a soft bed, and it was quiet. He pulled his paws from beneath the covers and pushed himself into a sitting position. The room around him was sterile but soft and warm, bathed in late morning sunlight. His tongue felt thick in his mouth, and a headache pounded between his ears with each heartbeat. A rustling noise beside him drew his attention to the chair on his left.

Kermodei sat quietly in the chair, his head resting on his large paws. Luteo was surprised to see Kermodei's eyes following his every move as he regained consciousness. Kermodei leaned back and placed his paws on the arms of the chair.

"How are you feeling, Luteolus?" Kermodei asked, his eyes pensive and sharp.

"Isabell…. Where is Isabell?" Luteo moved as if to rise from the bed but was struck by a cramp in his side.

"Rest, Luteolus. I'm afraid there is nothing we can do now." Kermodei's eyes moved from Luteo and stared out into the bright sunlight. "Your injuries are minor. Thank Tarsus that you were not but five paces closer to the stage and we would not be here now."

Luteo felt his face grow hot and tears well from his eyes.

"Thanks Tarsus? How could you possibly be thankful? Isabell is gone, and I couldn't do anything to save her." Luteo's paws curled into fists grasping the blankets. His breathing was heavy and wet. "Where is her body? I need to see her."

Kermodei stayed quiet and stroked the long grey hairs beneath his jawline.

"Once the Liberalia begins, Luteo, those participating cannot leave except in death or dishonor. And I promised your parents that I wouldn't let you leave in either." Kermodei sighed. "Trust me when I say this Luteo. You will have the rest of your life to grieve. You need to focus and make it through the Liberalia. Become the Ursa that your parents and I want you to become." Luteo gripped the sheets even tighter and clenched his jaw.

"How can you say this, Kermodei? Are you devoid of empathy or emotion? This is my sister we're talking about. I was watching her read by the fireplace less than a day ago!" Luteo growled, his voice thick with rage.

"You've been unconscious for the last three days. We're over seven hundred clicks away at the Liberalia grounds. We had no choice but to bring you with us, and the quickest way for you to get back to Isabell is by participating in the Liberalia," Kermodei explained in an even voice.

Luteo was silent, tears running down his face and wetting his fur. The silence stretched from a few seconds to a few minutes. Kermodei waited with his arms crossed while Luteo mulled over his limited choices.

"You give me one option Kermodei. I hate you for this, but what other choice do I have?" Luteo muttered through a clenched jaw.

Kermodei leaned forward and nodded in silence. He pulled himself to his feet and paced towards the door on the far side of the room. Kermodei opened it and Pern spilled out onto the floor, apparently trying his hardest to eavesdrop through the door. Pern jumped to his feet and ran over to Luteo.

"Luteo! I'm so sorry. Are you hurt? How are you?" Pern stumbled over his words, pulling at the sheets to make sure his friend was still in one piece. "Kermodei wouldn't let me see you until you woke up."

Luteo found himself overwhelmed by his friend's emotion, which was especially touching after Kermodei's cold and methodical council. Luteo grabbed Pern's arm and pulled him into an embrace, wincing when Pern squeezed his bruised sides.

"I love you Pern. And I'm going to need your support these next few days." Luteo sounded muffled while he spoke into Pern's furry shoulder. "Isabell is dead, and I have to push that aside. We need to get through the Liberalia as quick as we can and get home to Berarbor. I'll need you with me."

Pern pulled back from his friend's embrace and nodded while staring into Luteo's eyes.

"Well let's get you on your feet. I need to get you to our campsite and unpacked before the Liberalia's first trial tomorrow morning."

Luteo looked up at Pern and ground his teeth.

"For Isabell," Luteo stated. Pern looked down at him and grabbed Luteo's forearm.

"For Isabell."

Naka

As his grandmother predicted, Naka's father was home just in time for dinner. Naka peppered him with questions as soon as he got home, but his father insisted on eating together first. As a family rule, he would always say it was important to nourish the body before one could nourish the mind with important conversation. Privately, Naka suspected he actually was always too hungry to do anything but eat right when he got home. The meal did not feature the special glaze that Naka's grandmother picked up from his mother, but it was delicious nonetheless. With the events of the afternoon so clearly on everyone's mind, conversation at the table was sparse that evening. They served the food; they ate the food; they cleared the table. When they had finished dinner, Naka's grandmother got up from her seat and went for a convenient walk outside.

Naka spoke first. "Dad, how long have you been planning that? You said in the crowd that you've been speaking with connections in other Nakai towns and even in Kalani on the coast. Why did you hide all of that from me? How did you hide it from me?"

His father paused to reflect and then cleared his throat. "I hid my plans and my actions from you because telling you of my plans would have endangered you. I had to wait until I was sure that we could carry out the plans with faith that they could come to fruition. I trusted you to keep these secrets safe, but if someone else had found out about them—someone like Boto—I wanted you to have the ability to truthfully say that you had no idea what I was planning."

Naka shook his head. "I see what you're saying. But do you really think Boto or any of the other overseers or magistrates would have believed that I didn't know? Or would have cared at all? They would have made an example out of our whole family for what you did. I could have helped you."

Naka swallowed and then continued. "Last night you said that we could fight back against them, but that we had to do it in a smart, controlled way. Kill them with kindness, right? But then you go and jump up in front of the whole village and declare war on the Yamahito and the overseers. Is that not a reckless fight?"

His father nodded. "You're right, they would have punished you regardless. And yes, I see why my actions today do not make sense with what I said yesterday. I did plan to tell you soon, now that you've grown." He smiled. "The okolehao was my first step. I had planned to tell you in a few months' time, once the rice harvest had completed. Then the red sun happened. That sun is a very important symbol for our people. You see, a long, long time ago—before obachan's obachan was born—the elders of our people foretold the red sun. They did not say when it would occur, but they did say that when it did happen, it would usher in a great opportunity for our people. They never said explicitly what this opportunity would mean—I suppose they didn't want to push their luck with fortune telling. But they did foresee that we would revolt against the Yamahito. And I say that we have a real shot at winning. Kane's parents and I, and others in the village, have been planning for a rebellion for a while. We've been testing out the waters and making connections that can help us and band our people together. We had no way of knowing when the red sun would happen, or if it would even happen in our lifetimes. But until it did we could prepare for action, without tipping our hands, in the hopes that it would occur. Perhaps if we had to wait decades for the sun, we would have made a move without waiting. But the sun came today.

"That's why when I saw the sun turn crimson in the sky I went immediately to Kane's parents and we decided to unveil our plan and inspire our people to rebel. If we have any chance at all of bringing our culture and traditions back to our people, it's right now. The red sun is a symbol we can use to bring our people together. It will catalyze our people to action and begin a real resistance. But we cannot do everything from our village. We need to not only defend, but to go on the offensive as well. That's where you come in."

Naka's father placed a hand on Naka's shoulder. "When the Nakai elders long ago foretold of the red sun, they also gave a location. Our people are to send someone to a mountain very far away from here. It will be a long journey and, according to the elders, of crucial importance."

"And I am the one to go?" Naka asked. His father nodded. "Why me?"

"We have chosen you. Your grandmother and I, Kane's parents, and even the elders of our village. We know that we can trust you and depend on you to carry out this task."

"And what am I to do once I get to this mountain. What is the task?"

"That," Naka's father said, "we do not know. The elders were specific about many things, but they obscured much of what would be required—I presume to hide anything that could identify the end goal and reveal information sensitive to this mission."

"I do not understand." Naka shook his head. "I do not know enough. I only know how to plant and harvest rice—and I only barely know enough of that. How could I be responsible for whatever this task has of me?"

"Kanaka, listen to me." Naka stopped talking at the mention of his full name, which his family never used. "You do remember why we called you Kanaka, right?"

"It means 'human' in Nakai," Naka replied.

Naka's father nodded. "It's a reminder that no matter how people try to make you different, you will always be human, just like everyone else in Sokoku. You are not two separate halves. You are one whole. You have a unique perspective in our village. You have connections to both the Nakai and the Yamahito people. You've carried with you a perspective different from any other in our village, and you will use your perspective to make the decisions you need to make, whatever they be. You can help win people to our cause."

"We'll see." Naka thought for a few seconds. "So, I am to head to this mountain? When do you want me to go?"

"You must leave tonight. By early light tomorrow word of our gathering today will surely have reached the overseers and the lords who say they own these lands. Leaving tonight will put the most distance between you and them. While they are preoccupied with us here in the village, you will have none of their attention on your journey. But you are not heading straight to the mountain. First, you must travel to Kalani."

"The port city? There are no mountains near there."

"You're to travel there to meet a woman by the name of Shisuta. She will have something for you that you will need to bring to the mountain. You can find her in a tavern called Taizai."

"Who is this woman? One of your contacts in Kalani? Can we trust her?"

"Yes, I have known this woman for a very long time. I would trust her with my life, and you can trust her too. But you cannot trust anyone else that you meet on your journey. The empire is powerful and will do whatever it takes to hold onto its power. Although we are a small, inconsequential village in the eyes of the Yamahito, I have no doubt that Empress Karuto will hear of our demonstrations soon and will do everything she can to undermine our revolt. She will make an example of our village, Naka. Do not trust anyone besides Shisuta and those of us you know from the village."

Naka nodded. "I understand."

"Good. There's one other thing. Also in Kalani lives a wealthy and powerful Nakai man named Waiwai Kamoi. He proclaims himself to be the richest Nakai citizen in all of Sokoku, and knowing what I know of his wealth, I do not have reason to doubt the claim. See if you can track him down and speak with him. If we can win him to our cause, we will have a vast fortune available in our war chest. But Shisuta is your priority. Waiwai's aid would boost our rebellion, but Shisuta will provide you with far more crucial information. Now, best that you get ready. Pack what you can carry on you and meet me out front."

Naka nodded and left to his room to collect some things: an extra mapa, money for the road, some rice and dried fish for the start of the journey, and sandals that he wore when walking between towns. After a second to think, he also grabbed the bottle of okolehao on his way out. He had only gotten to taste it the one night, after all. When Naka came outside after collecting his things, he found his father and Kane waiting for him. Kane also had a rucksack with him and a silly, determined smile on his face.

"Kane, what are you doing here? You're coming too?"

"Well, I couldn't just let you go get into trouble without me, could I?"

"What about your parents? They'll need help here in the village with my dad."

Kane winked. "My parents are the ones who told me to get out of here and go with you. Apparently, they're worried you'll get into trouble without someone with a strong head on his shoulders at your side."

Naka's father nodded. "You'll have need of help on this journey, Naka. You and Kane have known each other since before you can remember. Working together you have a much better chance of reaching the mountain and surmounting the obstacles you may find on your way. Besides, you'll want someone to talk to on the journey and someone to help drink the okolehao that I'm betting you took with you," he said with a smile.

Naka smiled back and, with the sweetest voice he could muster, said "dad, I would never dream of taking your bottle. That would start our journey off on an ominous foot."

"Well," his father replied. "I bought the bottle so that both of you could try it, so you have my blessing if you do decide to take it with you."

"That's very generous of you, dad. The bottle may or may not be in my knapsack as we speak."

Naka's father laughed and pulled his son into a hug. When he pulled away moments later, he wiped tears from his eyes. "Naka, I am proud of the person you have become," he said, nodding to Kane as well. "I'm proud of both of you men. You've worked hard for our families in the fields and your work has paid off in the harvest we will bring in. Now you face an altogether different task, but one that you can accomplish with perseverance, strength, and determination. Do not forget that you have not only our families behind you, but you have our people behind you as well. All Nakai who want a nation to call their own support you and what you're doing." He looked up at the stars in the sky. "It's beginning to get late. I should not delay you much longer. You may leave after one last hug."

"I love you, dad," said Naka as he teared up in his father's arms. "Keep our rebellion alive but keep yourself safe too. I will need your guidance for many more years after I return, and we have many more shared drinks ahead of us."

"I love you too son. I will keep your grandmother out of trouble while we wait on you two to come home."

As they walked away, heading out of the only place that the two had ever known, they stopped several times to look back at the cluster of houses in Naka's corner of the village. "Seems crazy, doesn't it?" Kane said after one of the glances. "Last night we were drinking with your father. This morning we were working in the fields. Tonight, we're leaving our home for a city that we've never seen. At this rate, by this time tomorrow we'll have toppled the head of our government and next week we'll have died of old age after living long, peaceful lives and raising beautiful families."

Naka laughed. "Don't forget about the statues they'll have commissioned for us in every village square on the coast. Or about the riches we're sure to find on our journey."

Kane chuckled and then stopped walking for a moment. "Do you think we can make a difference for our people? Do you think our parent's revolution has a chance to succeed?"

"I do not know," Naka responded. "But I know that we have to at least try. Besides, now that our loving parents have decided to publicly oppose the Empire, prompting the state to most likely seize our fields and grant them to another, less aggravating family, we kind of have to trust that their plan will work out, don't we?"

"I suppose we do." Kane shook his head. "Man, I'm gonna need that drink as soon as we decide to stop."

Raban

Raban wiped his dry eyes and looked around. He was lying on the ground next to Navine, surrounded by the crowd of people, all looking away from them. Navine's white gown was covered in deep crimson stains. Blood dripped from her mouth. Her wings bent in an odd way. She was not moving.

"Navey, are you okay?" Raban asked.

She still didn't move. Raban rolled over and felt a surge of pain in his back as he pushed off the ground. He crawled over to her and examined her body; many of her wing feathers were ripped off and her legs had long deep gashes in them. There were dark red bald spots where it appeared the ants had eaten all the feathers and dug deep into the skin. He put his face to her beak and couldn't hear any breathing.

"Somebody, please help!" Raban called, looking around at the crowd, but nobody looked down at him. All eyes were pointed towards the sky, and people were whispering to each other.
"Ka'kaw! Can anybody hear me? Navine needs help. She is really hurt, and I don't think she is going to make it!"

Raban looked desperately around the crowd, yet no one responded. He stood up and grabbed the nearest monk and dragged him over to Navine.
"Can you please help her!"
"Well, there's nothing that can be done. Some just aren't' made for this rite, we have more important—"

Raban grabbed the monk by his long throat.
"How dare you! She saved my Huginn-damned life in there!"

He looked down at Navine's motionless body and grasped the monk's neck harder.

"Look… up…" gasped the monk and pointed to the sky.

Raban's eyes tracked his fingers toward the sun. He released his grasp, and the monk stumbled away. It was the first time he noticed where everyone else was looking. They were all staring at the sun.

It appeared as a ruby-red, majestic orb. The red circle reminded him of Navine's wounds. He looked down at Navine. Her body was lifeless.

I will save Muni. In Navine's name, I will wreak havoc on the Inlanders, Raban thought to himself.

Suddenly, the sun's color changed. The deep red color vanished, and everyone turned away, shading their eyes with their wings. The sun was no longer a fiery red orb but once again an eye-burning bright ball.

Raban reached down and held Navine's hand. It was ice cold. He pushed back her face feathers and kissed her on the forehead.

When he stood up, the crowd of Arborns were all looking at him.

"It is a sign from the King Raven himself that Raban Mellori is our chosen one!" cried someone in the crowd, who stepped forward.

Raban recognized this individual; it was the Lord Mayor of Arbornesta, Freya Folligna.

"Ka'kaw, for his sister's sake, he will end the dreaded era of the Inlanders!" responded one of the monks.

The Lord Mayor nodded and stepped forward. "Yes, this boy has proven himself in many ways today. His love and courage will be remembered in the canopies for many seasons to come. Your friend Navine's sacrifice will also not be forgotten. You are all heroes to us." She gestured toward Navey's body and him. "I believe that the Red Sun was no accident. And as Lord Mayor, I request that you follow what our great spiritual leader, Vali, is about to tell you. You are a special bird, Raban, and you have a special mission. I thank you and your family's continued dedication to our people."

The surrounding crowd applauded.

"Thank you, Lord Mayor" mumbled Raban, slightly confused by the situation.

Great Leader Vali stepped up next to her and greeted him with a slight bow.

"My son. You are a true Mellori boy. Not only did you survive, but you, like your ancestors, have found a way to make life more interesting for all of us," he said with a large grin. "The sun decided to greet you with a special welcome to adulthood. Congratulations on this success. You are now a full-grown Arborn."

Vali stepped closer and greeted Raban with a traditional mature wing touch. Raban responded and touched inner wing feathers with Vali. Raban could only imagine how much his father would love to see this moment.

"Thank you, Great Leader, it is a great honor to hear these kind words from you, and from Lord Mayor."

"Of course, my son. For any Arborn with eyes, it is clear that adventure flows through your blood, like your mother and father. Instead of exploring for your own pleasure or gain, though, I want you to harness that energy for your people, for your sister, for Navine. I believe that the King Raven's spirit wants you to go to Chasteria with the guidance of my closest Huginn warriors and bring bloodshed to those who have wronged you and our people."

Vali clapped, and a dozen tall muscular Arborns stepped forward. All carrying traditional forest slings and thuma shields.

"You will lead a mission for all of us. So, do not only return with your sister, but also bring pain to any noble Inlander you see—especially the kraven king, Lord Chasta. He has caused our people pain, and we should do the same. You should kidnap Lord Chasta's niece, Emilia if you can. I think it will do good to remind the Inlanders that there are consequences when they attack our people in our own forest! The Red Sun has chosen you to be an Arborn warrior and bring justice to the land!"

The crowd erupted in thunderous applause. Raban nodded but felt a weird tension in his wing muscles.

Kill Inlander nobles? Kidnap some young girl? I want to save Muni, but this mission wasn't what I imagined...

Vali continued saying, "You will bring honor to all our people, Raban. Try and get some rest now because you and my warriors will head out tonight at twilight. We have a few secrets up our sleeves. By the end of the night, you should be reunited with your sister."

With those final words, Vali put his white cloak back over his head and walked away.

"Best of luck my dear boy. Don't forget to bring back Emilia," said Lord Mayor Freya with a sharp grin, as she turned and followed Vali.

Two Huginn monks stepped by Raban and picked up Navine's body and started to carry her away.

"Wait, what are you two doing" called Raban and turned to grab one of them by the wing. "We are taking her to the temple tree. Great Leader told us to hold her there in the trunk until you return, and then we will honor her with the final Burning rite."

Raban was speechless. The Burning rite was reserved for fallen heroes, and honored elders. For Navine to receive this last reserved rite reflected a great deal of respect.

He could only nod and let go of the monk's wing. He pulled out one of Navine's inner feathers as they carried her body away. Raban's head and heart ached. It was only yesterday that they were chatting at his doorway.

Luteo

The Liberalia grounds were nestled between two large hills that marked the subtle transition of the flatlands into the mountains, placed in the geographical center of Berarbor, Terrarctos, and Ursolympa. The forest thickened out to the northeast, shading the path that they had followed to arrive at the grounds. Terrarctos was to the southeast and barely visible— the only hint was a lack of topography and a flat horizon. Ursolympa was directly to the west, evidenced by thorny mountains that tore at the western sky. Each year the migration of young Ursa from Berarbor into the ceremonial site brought life and noise into the region, awakening the grounds from their silent slumber.

Directly in the center of the grounds, stood a ring of ancient stones that acted as an amphitheater for those attending the Liberalia. Luteo found himself standing next to Pern and the rest of the Ursa from Berarbor in the darkness of early morning. It was hard to make out the figures on the far side of the ring, but Luteo remembered Pern telling him the Olympa and Terrera sat opposite them, each group closest to their geographical origin. Kermodei was easier to see, as he stood in the center of the ring to lead the ceremony.

"Terrera. Arbora. Olympa." Kermodei spoke in a slow and clear voice. "It is impossible with these divisions to remember what you truly are. You are Ursa and you have forgotten it." Kermodei turned in a circle, surveying the obvious division among the young Ursa.

Kermodei raised both of his arms and continued turning.

As he had been instructed earlier, Luteo got to his feet and mixed among the rest of the Ursa, shuffling between Terrera and Olympa alike. He found himself on the far side, sitting next to an unusually large dark Ursa from Olympa. He looked down at Luteo and smiled.

"My name is Eremicus. You can call me Erem," the large Ursa whispered through his teeth.

"Luteolus. My friends call me Luteo." Luteolus reached out with his paw and grasped Erem's. They locked eyes and then looked back to Kermodei who was waiting for silence from the murmuring youth. A flurry of activity caught Luteo's eye, and he looked past Kermodei to see the same familiar Ursa from the Terrera entrance ceremony back in Berarbor – bone-white fur and dark rings around his eyes – pushing a small Ursa from Olympa seated next to him. The large Ursa seemed to be enjoying his molestation of the smaller Ursa, grinning with a sick gleam in his eye as he pushed her repeatedly. She kept her eyes trained forward and tried to ignore him.

Kermodei cleared his throat. The dark-eyed Ursa turned back forward and continued smiling as he stopped harassing his neighbor. Luteo felt an unsettling churn in his stomach as he saw the lack of remorse or empathy in those ringed eyes.

"Your neighbors are all Ursa just like you, but they have an entirely separate meaning of the words 'home' and 'family'. You may remember the sweeping expanse of the flatlands of Terrarctos, or the craggy pathways of Ursolympus. You may have 10 siblings and you may have none. The only thing we know for certain is that you are different.

"That is why we are here. We are here to learn from our neighbors, to burn out our misconceptions of each other and to celebrate that which makes us unique. To do so, there are three trials you must pass." Kermodei paused and looked out in the early-morning darkness. He held up his right paw.

"The Trial of the Right Claws. The Trial of the Body. We will have a series of obstacles to further get you in tune with the vessel that holds you." Kermodei held out his left paw.

"The Trial of the Left Claws. The Trial of the Mind. You will face your greatest fears in your own way. We've gathered information from those closest to you to isolate your deepest worries—and we will bring them to life before your eyes. Will you overcome?" Kermodei paused, then joined his two paws together over his heart.

"The Trial of the Inner Claws. Each of you will have an entirely different manifestation of this trial. For some of you it will require little sacrifice. For others…" Kermodei paused, and locked eyes with Luteo.

"With that, I would like to call for the commencement of the Trials. We will begin at precisely noon." Kermodei pushed his arms forward to point to the flatlands in the east. At the exact moment his arms came to a stop, a deep red light burst over the horizon and filled the valley.

Bathed in a blood-red light, gasps echoed throughout the ring. Luteo had never seen a sun with such a complex and vibrant shade of maroon. It had to be more than just a normal sunrise. Luteo turned his gaze back to Kermodei and was shocked to see that even Kermodei seemed to be unsettled. Maybe this red sun wasn't part of the Liberalia after all? Kermodei gaped at the sun without speaking, and the entire valley seemed to come to a standstill under the bloody morning rays shining from the east.

After what felt like ten minutes, Kermodei jerked to a start and cleared his throat. He looked around at the ring of young Ursa and found Luteo among the circle. His eyes lingered for a moment and he gave a brief nod. Luteo had no idea what the nod or significant glance meant and shuffled in his seat.

"This is a most unusual event," Kermodei spoke in an even voice. "The red sun hasn't graced our kingdens for the last few hundred years. You are all part of something very special." Kermodei shuffled off the dais in the center of the ring and made his way to the tents on the northern side of the encampment.

"At the stroke of noon, we begin."

***

The peculiar red sun was almost at its zenith, and the Ursa congregated a few clicks from the ring of stones at the ground's center. A gigantic wooden door was mounted into the hillside, with archaic markings running down the front. Kermodei stood at the front of the group, leading them to an empty clearing at the base of the door. Luteo had donned his Arbora cloak and marked the fur on both cheeks with dark maroon powder from the dogberry trees back at home. Pern walked with him in perfect pace, also wearing his cloak but instead ornamented with the deep blue streaks of the dried iris flowers. Luteo's new friend Erem walked behind the two of them, carrying the traditional pickstaff of the Olympa. Designed for picking ore from sheer mountain cliffs, Erem seemed more comfortable carrying it with him during such an uncertain and nerve-wracking trial.

Kermodei reached the last section of the clearing closest to the wooden doors and stopped in his tracks. The doors had seemed large from afar but kept growing as they approached and appeared to be over 25 Ursa tall. The young Ursa spread in a semicircle around Kermodei and sat to listen to the rules of the trial.

"Beyond these doors are the same obstacles that your parents and their parents faced, all the way back to the earliest Ursa." Gesturing up to the doors, Kermodei paced in a loose circle while he surveyed his pupils.

"Look around you. Among you are your peers and friends, but also your rivals." Luteo scanned the Ursa sitting among him, finding most of the others following suit. "You will enter the doors alone, but inside the maze that you find ahead, you will face one of your peers. There are no rules during the final sparring section of the Trial of the Right Claws. The will of Tarsus can be both cruel and kind, but the nature you find will be entirely up to fate."

Kermodei paused. "You must use your body and your strength for this trial. There are to be no weapons or tools." Erem snorted and placed his pickstaff behind him.

"Who will be first?" Kermodei asked the group.

"Me." grunted the eye-ringed Ursa as he got to his feet. He strode forward to the center of the semicircle and bowed to Kermodei. "My name is Titanus, son of Denmaster Arcos. I will lead the way for my peers, and I will show them how it is done." Titanus looked back at his snickering friends from Terrarctos and winked in a theatrical flair.

"So be it," grumbled Kermodei. He led Titanus to the base of the wooden doors that towered above them and place his hand on the seam between the two. With a very light touch, Kermodei pushed on the seam. A large shuddering noise echoed from the door hinges, as the gap between the doors widened to the exact berth of an average Ursa. Kermodei stepped back and gestured for Titanus to enter.

Titanus inhaled and paused for a moment, before throwing himself into the cavern before him. The semi-circle was silent for a few minutes, as if everyone expected Titanus to exit in tears. Kermodei broke the silence.

"Who is next?" Luteolus waited while a dozen anxious Ursa preceded him. He felt anxious but prepared – if every adult he knew back home had done this, he was confident that he could do it to. His only hope was that he faced a reasonable foe at the end of the tunnel.

Pern elbowed Luteo in the side and whispered, "Get up there, you cub-brain." Luteo snickered and rose to his feet. Kermodei looked over to Luteo and smiled.

"I was wondering when you might stand up," Kermodei mused, and held an arm out for Luteo. Luteo approached and stared into the deep abyss looming before him. Kermodei leaned over and whispered into Luteo's ear, "Stay alive in there Luteo. I'm afraid I have something I need to tell you tonight."

Luteo could hardly register what Kermodei said. He felt as if the cold black nothingness ahead of him drew him in, calling for his warmth.

Before he could give it a second thought, Luteo stepped forward and disappeared from the light.

Naka

Naka and Kane walked from village to village, following the large road that would lead them south and eventually to Kalani. The two were used to standing all day working in the fields, and they had traveled to other nearby towns before to sell their rice, but those experiences fell short of preparing them for days on the road. They stopped at each village to buy or trade supplies, but for good measure opted to camp each night rather than spend the night in places they did not know. Word of the rebellion in Manaolana had traveled fast, somehow beating them to every town. Naka figured that the connections his dad had made had helped the news travel as quickly as it did. They were careful not to ask too many questions about the rebellion so as not to raise suspicion, but they found that often they did not have to ask many questions at all. The rebellion was the hot topic of conversation in each place they went, and they saw that most of the people they met were cautiously supportive of the people in Manaolana.

After three nights on the road, the two finally reached Kalani. Even from miles away, the city was unlike anything that either of them had seen: as wide as any mountain and much taller than the tallest palm trees found in Manaolana. From the gently rolling hills surrounding the city, they saw an enormously intricate system of wooden ports with what must have been nearly a thousand ships either at port or moving about in the bay. As they approached the city limits, they could hear chatter and the cacophony of crowds that would never fit in the village they knew, with merchants and shoppers shouting at each other to haggle down prices. Once inside the city, they discovered that it was also more diverse than their home. Nakai comprised the majority of the population—it was a coastal city after all— but there were many more Yamahito than Naka had ever seen in one place.

As they walked through the streets it was also clear how much more opulent the general population was than in Manaolana. People wore similar clothes and styles, but the fabrics looked much nicer and more durable. They had higher quality footwear and looked thicker in the bones, too. Naka also noticed guards standing at attention every so often and saw that they wore long, thin, silver swords strapped to their waists. Boto's henchmen carried the same style of swords too.

Wandering through the city, weaving between bustling people and buildings that loomed much closer together than they were used to, Naka and Kane stopped an older Nakai woman to ask where they could find the center of town.

"New to town, eh?" she said with a smile. "You can get to downtown if you follow this street further down for about two miles. If you're looking for a place to stay though, most of the inns will be away from the center, about a mile that way if you take a right," she said, pointing down a large avenue filled with merchant stalls and chattering crowds.

Naka and Kane thanked her for her help and took the street to the right toward the inn. While they didn't stay overnight in any of the other villages they passed, Kalani was much, much larger than they anticipated and they realized they might need a few days to find the woman they sought.

Once inside their rented room, for which they had to pay up front with nearly half of the money they had left, they were happy to see that the beds were already turned with the foot of each bed facing away from the doorway to make sure that their spirits didn't escape the room as they slept. They sat on their beds and took a breath. "This city is insane," Kane let out with a wide-eyed look. "How do all of these people live with these crowds? How do they get where they're going without getting lost or trampled? I feel like we narrowly avoided death multiple times out there."

Naka nodded. "This place is nothing like I've ever seen. Did you see how many different types of food some of those stalls had? Each week if you could only eat food you'd never tasted before, you'd still never die of hunger."

"And the roads—mostly stone! That stone must have taken ages to set."

"This city has more people than I've ever seen in my entire life. There must be dozens of women named Shisuta."

"But we can start with the Taizai place your father mentioned. The innkeeper here may know where it is. This Waiwai Kamoi person, on the other hand, could prove harder to track. Hopefully a Nakai man of untold riches is as rare and recognition-worthy here as it would be in our village, otherwise we may not be able to find him."

They located the innkeeper on the first floor of the building trying to hang a large painting in the hall with the help of two kids a few years younger than Naka. He dropped his side of the painting and let out a loud curse in Yamahito before then cursing at the boys trying to help him, who, like the innkeeper, looked Nakai. When Naka and Kane approached him from behind, he startled and snapped at them as well, before catching himself and apologizing.

"Excuse me, sir," Kane said. "We're looking for a bar called Taikai. Do you know it?"

"Know it? Yeah, but I'd never set foot in it. Place is heavy with Yamahito most of the time. Heard it's not always so friendly to people like us. If you want a drink, I'd go to Yote Tengoku instead. Much friendlier atmosphere and all the okolehao you could want." Kane and Naka exchanged glances.

"Thank you, but we're meeting a friend at Taikai."

"Some friend. Your call." The innkeeper bent down to pick up the painting again. "Walk out the door to your left and then take your first right and you'll find Taikai Tavern about a mile down the road."

Naka and Kane thanked him for his help and followed his instructions down the avenue. Halfway through their walk, Kane stopped Naka at the side of the road. "Have you noticed that as we've walked, this street has had fewer and fewer Nakai and more and more Yamahito? Isn't this city supposed to be majority Nakai?"

Naka looked around and saw that he did indeed see mostly Yamahito folk walking around, some of them staring in their direction. "It is majority Nakai. Maybe it's like the part of Manaolana that Boto and the other overseers live in? The only time that row of houses has a single drop of Nakai blood is when one of the overseers comes back a little dirty from shaking down some poor farmers."

Kane nodded. "Let's make sure to get in and out of this place quick and not get into any shit with these people while we do it."

By the time they reached the tavern, they could no longer identify any Nakai on the road or at the shopping stalls that lined the sides of the street. The building itself was nothing special from the outside, a two-story structure with a couple of modestly sized windows overlooking the road. Little decoration went into the sign swinging over their heads, which simply printed *Taikai* in broad, lazy strokes. Gulping, the two turned to each other and then to the front door and went inside.

When they entered, it seemed as though every pair of eyes in the entire place settled on them immediately. The chatter in the room noticeably quieted for the slightest moment, but then most of the people went back to talking and drinking. They sidled over to the bar, careful not to knock anyone's drink along the way. The bartender was the largest Yamahito man he had ever seen and was close to the largest man he had seen even among the Nakai. They watched the walls, or the floor, or anything else that wasn't him as he took orders from the other patrons sitting at the bar. After fifteen minutes or so, when the bartender saw that they indeed were still waiting there, he came over.

"You two here for a drink? A lot of other places you could go that would have a friendlier clientele."

"Oh, but we like the welcoming atmosphere here—much more our speed," Kane said, his voice trailing off toward the end of the sentence when he saw that it wasn't landing with the enormous man in front of them.

"What my friend means to say is we're here looking for someone. A woman by the name of Shisuta."

The bartender leaned away from the bar and took a step back at the mention of the woman's name. "You two know—" he cut himself off. "Here, let me pour you two some soku." He took a large brown bottle, shaped differently from the bottle of okolehao Naka had back in their room, and aimed heavy pours into two ceramic glasses. He pushed the two drinks across the wooden surface to the two visitors and snapped his fingers at a kid a couple years their junior who was standing upright against the wall behind them

"Yoshinabe, take these two to the room in the back and tell Miss Hageshi that she has visitors."

They followed the silent young man through a door at the other end of the bar and down a long hallway that changed direction three times, past several unmarked doors, until they reached a formidable rosewood door with an ornate copper handle. He opened the door with a key and then gestured for them to enter the room. Naka and Kane exchanged a glance but went inside nevertheless. He closed the door after them. They looked at the door handle for a nervous moment but did not hear the lock click behind them.

After around thirty minutes of stillness interspersed with idle chatter, someone knocked at the door. "Um, come in?" Naka said. The door swung slowly open to reveal a Yamahito woman of average height and build and in her middle years. She wore a silky robe on which light shapes vaguely resembling fish overlaid cool shades of blue. Naka noted her eyes, which seemed to cut into the two of them with ease. "And to whom do I owe this unexpected visit?" Though her inflection suggested she was asking, her expression and demeanor let them know it was more of a command than a request.

"Well, Miss Hageshi," Naka started. "We were actually under the impression that this visit was expected. My father, Kawika Pikala, sent me a long way to come see you."

Shisuta took half a step back before quickly regaining her composure, but Naka could tell her demeanor had changed completely. In a warmer tone, she asked, "You're Kawika's son?"

"Yes, madam, I am. So, you do know him?"

Her eyes lit up as she smirked. "I should hope that I do. He eloped with my sister many years ago."

Raban

He walked back to his family's nest alone with his heavy pack, his talon necklace, bloodstained polespear, and Navine's wing feather. When he opened the door, and stepped down his family's mossy steps, the sadness and fear about the whole situation started to sink in. He looked into Muni's empty sleeping corridor and thought about her big soulful eyes on that small round face. He had failed his family and now he had one shot to make it right. He grabbed some water and his father's sharpening stone and started to clean his polespear and sharpen the edge of the blade. It felt like a lifetime ago when he killed the Giant River Otter with this blade. As he moved his wings, cleaning the spear, his whole body ached. His head pulsed, his back stung, his legs itched, and his chest throbbed.

As he sat in the corner remembering all the sources of pain, he heard some movement from his parent's sleeping chamber.

Raban forgot about his pain and stood up. His heart pounded. He was ready for a fight. Out from his parent's doorway stepped an older Corvidean. Her eyes beamed kindness and her feathers looked soft and downtrodden. She looked like she knew herself well.

"Ka'kaw, Raban, I've been waiting for you."

"Uh, Ka'kaw" Raban said, looking her up and down. "Sorry to ask, but who are you? and what are you doing here?"

The older lady chuckled and sat down next to Raban.

"You really don't know who I am? Well I thought you were supposed to be staying at my place, so I could ask you the same question. Why you are still here?"

"Great Auntie?" asked Raban,

"So, you do remember me. Well I'm happy to hear I didn't waste all those years coughing up Slange meat for you and Muni when you were both just little featherless younglings," she said with a warm smile.

"I'm sorry Great Auntie! It's been quite some time, and the past couple days have not gone exactly as I planned. I don't know how to say this, but Muni was kidnapped."

Great Auntie was nodding her head and didn't seem surprised.

"Yes, yes, so I've heard," she said. "We have quite a few topics to discuss. I hope you are ready for everything that I have to share."

The skin around Raban's eyes flushed red. His forehead pulsed even harder. "Great Auntie, I don't know what you've heard, but you don't seem very concerned about my sister right now. I have a mission from the Great Leader to go save her and a small army at my back. I don't really care about whatever other personal or family drama you want to discuss right

now. I think I have a bit more pressing topics on hand." Raban said and
turned away from her. He started to wipe his blade clean again with water
and sharpen it with his father's stone.

"Well, you sure do have the stubbornness of a Mellori," laughed
Great Auntie.

Raban did not look up from the blade and pushed the stone harder
and harder against the spear. His fingers slipped and two of them sliced
open on the blade. "Kaw!" Raban jumped up in pain.

"Oh, let me help you with that," said Great Auntie as she pulled
out a cloth from her bag and leaned towards him, but Raban stepped away
and walked over to his pack.

"I'm fine," he spurted as he paced back and forth from his pack,
holding tight his cut fingers.

A slapping sound of something spongy caused both Raban and his
Great Auntie to turn around to face the corner where Raban's pack sat.

Next to it, there sat a thick, brown, squishy creature.

"What is that thing?" asked Great Auntie.

Raban eyes grew wide. It was the same Mudskap that he had found
near the river!

"What in Huginn's name are you doing here?" asked Raban.

"Well, friend, I guess I might have listened to a few things that you
said. So, when I saw what happened to you and your sister, I thought you
might need some help. Also, the fact that my house was destroyed was a bit
of an incentive to move somewhere new," said the Mudskap and hopped
over to Raban.

"Yeah, again I'm sorry about that," replied Raban.

"You are getting pretty good at these apologies. Now let me see
this new cut of yours."

Raban put his hand down and the Mudskap hopped up onto his
palm and started licking the cuts with his long tongue. Almost instantly, the
cuts stopped bleeding and Raban started to feel a tingling sensation in his
fingers. The wounds began to heal themselves! Raban couldn't believe it.

"Not too bad of a lunch for me, but I have to say you always taste
a bit salty," said the Mudskap as he finished licking and hopped off Raban's
hand.

"Wait, did you clean my wounds after Muni and I were attacked?"
asked Raban.

"No, it was the other Mudskap that has been following you
around," the Mudskap said and rolled its eyes. Great Auntie giggled.

"Well thank you, friend. What was your name again?"

"Your thick tongue and long beak would never be able to
pronounce it. Let's stick to something you can say: just call me Mudskap."

"Alright, Mudskap. My name is Raban. It's good to meet you."

"Yup, yup, and who's this bird lady? Should I leave? Does she like eating Mudskap legs?"

"Well no," Raban said, "but regardless, I think she was just leaving." Raban glanced over at his Great Auntie, who was sitting in his mom's chair.

"That's enough, Rabe," replied Great Auntie. She stood up and walked toward Mudskap. "Hi there, friend. My name is Kit. I'm pretty sure I met your mother. Was her name—" The following sounds that came out of Great Auntie's mouth sounded less like words to Raban and more like a tree Slange slithering through crunchy dried leaves.

"She was quite an amazing lady," his Great Auntie continued. "Not as feisty as you, but she was also an incredible healer like yourself."

Mudskap's mouth dropped open, and he glanced quickly between Raban and Great Aunt Kit. "You bird people continue to surprise me," he said. "What can I do to help you?"

"Before you arrived, Mudskap, I was about to explain to my grand-nephew some very important information about a very important quest. If you feel interested in joining on this journey, then stick around. If not, please head back to your river bank so we can have some privacy," Great Auntie said with a knowing smile.

"Ah, you won't get rid of me that easy, so just lay it out," replied Mudskap, his eyes flickering with excitement.

"Well before I begin, let me start over to you, Raban." She turned to look at Raban. "You know I love you and your sister, and when she was kidnapped, so was a part of my heart. I knew you would return here so I also returned here, but everything changed when the Red Sun appeared. This sign hasn't shone like that in many, many years, but we've been waiting patiently for it. We knew that it was finally time for the quest."

"Wait, who is this 'we'?" asked Raban, arching his wings forward.

"We will get there soon enough. Now, it's true that the Red Sun was the signal for the Chosen One to arise and go off on their mission, but not the mission that you were given by Vali. Our Chosen One has been in the Mellori family for many generations, and whoever holds that," she said, pointing to the talon on Raban's neck, "at the time of the next Red Sun is the Chosen One."

"Wait, but I'm not the Chosen One, this talon is my father's—"

"—Yes, I know who the talon used to belong to, but that does not matter. Look at the talon. What do you see?"

Raban examined the talon. Its sharp black curve shimmered with slight inset grooves on its sides. At the base, Raban saw a carved symbol. He wondered how he could have missed it. It was an emblem of the Red Sun.

"See? It only matters who has rightful possession of the talon at the time of the Red Sun, and right now it appears to be you. Your Mother and Father had to go on an important mission for the Resistance in the Western lands that lie along the Vast Sea. They are now two days in that direction, and even if they saw the Red Sun, they know it is your responsibility now that you have the talon."

"So, my parents are not going to Ringer's Bay? And what is this Resistance? Resistance to what?"

"Oh goodness, no my child, they never would go to that boring spot." Great Auntie's soft face feathers bounced as she laughed.

"Those tales of our family travel have been distorted for the outsiders' ears. We can't let those who want to know actually know where we are going. We have always had to hide our real motives and actions. Luckily, our travels have brought us much knowledge and wealth, which has given your parents a nice covering for their 'worldly travel,' but in reality, this travel has all been connected to the Resistance. And who is this Resistance? Well they are a loose network of believers, travelers, and fighters from around Godsdorf, all committed to seeking the Truth and stopping anyone that want to oppress us. Now, it is your turn to do your part. When you go on your mission to save Muni, I will guide you to meet up with some other Resistance fighters in the city of Chasteria, and there you and Muni can escape. However, you cannot return here, but you must continue the mission. Together, with the help of Mudskap, you will continue beyond the Inland city and go towards Mt. Vesus. In the valley in front of the giant volcano, there is a small, cold, blue lake. Wait there. Others from the Resistance all around Godsdorf will meet you at the lake. You should learn more once you reach the lake, but for now, that is all I know."

Raban wasn't sure what to say. His lungs flattened; he couldn't seem to get enough air no matter how hard he breathed in. All this information made his life a lot more complicated. He was already frightened by his mission to save Muni, and now somehow this unknown Resistance group that survived generations was depending on him, his sister, and Mudskap. His parents were members of this group too and were on a separate mission. It all sounded like a dream.

"So, I'm still going to save my sister first, right?" Raban said with some hesitation.

"Of course. Your sister is being held prisoner by some very evil people. We want to fight injustice, and this is a clear example of it. But once you save her, you must keep going. This injustice is not alone out there in Godsdorf. There is a great deal. We must not rest with this step. You must journey to the lake and help the Resistance fight more injustice that has spread across our land. I know you are still young, but do you think you are strong enough for that?"

Raban's face flushed a deep ruby color, and his face feathers creased into a sharp angle. "Of course, I'm ready for anything!"

"Good—and just in case you aren't," Great Auntie said as she smiled and walked over to put a small bag in his pack.

"Anyway, once you reach the city, you will need to go to the tallest guard tower on the eastside of the city. There will be a friend of the Resistance there. He will show you how to get to the lake. But I think it's time for you to start on this journey. Look outside: it's already dusk." Great Auntie was right; the time had flown by and nightfall was upon them.

"Well, Great Auntie, I don't know what to say. Thank you for your honesty. I will remember your words."

"Of course, Raban. And don't forget to tell Muni how much I miss her when you see her. Good luck, my sweet nephew."

"Thanks, Great Auntie, will do. Ready, Mudskap?"

"I don't know about you, but after all this exciting talk, I'm ready for a nap," Mudskap said with a yawn as he hopped up into Raban's pack. "Wake me up when we get somewhere important."

Raban picked up his pack with Mudskap and grabbed his polespear. He gave his Great Auntie a small head nod as he stepped outside into the twilight.

Outside he could hear some movement on the groundfloor. Below the bridge outside of his house, he saw the twelve warriors sent by Vali. All rode gigantic 5-horned rhinos. The same animals as the Inlanders. Raban thought this was a bit odd. He peeked over the edge and made eye contact with one of the taller warriors.

"The sleepy youngling has finally wandered out from his family's nest!" cried one of the warriors, and the rest laughed. This warrior's face feathers were all shaved off and his bald head shined red in the sunset.

"Get down here before we ride off!" called another warrior, who was holding onto an extra rhinoback. He looked like one of the younger ones, and his beak was open and smiling at Raban.

Without hesitation, Raban jumped and glided down, landing only a few feet from them.

"Flawless descent, youngling. Now stop showing off. We have ground to make up. Do you know how to ride one of these things?" called the bald warrior.

Raban looked the large beast up and down. Its horns were sharper than he expected, and its hairy nostrils were pierced with a sharp ring with ropes riding up its back. Snot trickled down its snout. The rhino stared Raban down.

STEVIE B. B. KING

"Of course," replied Raban and tried to swing up on the back. The rhino bucked forward tossing him and his pack onto the ground.

All the warriors laughed at the sight. The one closest to him whispered, "Don't worry, but this time grab those ropes first and give it a slight tug, it will remind the rhino who's boss."

Raban's back feathers were covered in dry leaves, and his throat felt even drier than them, but he listened and pulled himself up with a small tug on the ropes. The rhino stayed still, and he tied his pack on its back with ease.

"Alright, the fresh meat finally figured it out. Let's ride!" cried the bald leader and kicked his talons into the rhino's back. It sped off through the underbrush.

"Hold on tight, friend, and give the beast a good kick!" said the younger one next to him as he kicked off.

"Here we go!" Raban called to Mudskap and kicked hard with his talons. The beast roared and sped off behind the elite warriors of Arbornesta.

94

Luteo

Luteo was surrounded by void. As his eyes began to adjust, he saw shapes through the chamber, slight differences in the shades of grey that indicated the edges and ridges of objects in the room. Closing his eyes, Luteo drew on his other senses to give him an understanding of his surroundings. He heard a slight whistling as wind flowed past him from behind his shoulders into the darkness ahead. Echoes bounced off the walls around him, reverberating through the cavernous hallway. He smelled the dank rot that is reserved for places often enclosed in humid darkness.

Luteo opened his eyes and the room was clearer to him. A deep cavern stretched out before him, around one hundred paces directly into the solid rock of the cliffs. Hundreds of black archways punctured the stone walls surrounding him, appearing every few paces. Luteo was unable to notice a difference in any of the doorways—this must be the first choice to make in the Trial.

Walking past the doorways, Luteo tried to smell for fresh air. He scoured the floor before each doorway for disruptions in the decades of dust that had accumulated. Making out a few scuffs in the dust ahead, Luteo continued for a few moments. The tracks stopped mid-pace, with no apparent doorways in front of them. Blowing air out of his nostrils in a quick snort, Luteo turned in a slow circle, and then picked an archway on the left side of the wall.

Luteo almost tripped on the first stair. Recessed just behind the entryway into the arch, the stairway burst out of the ground and led Luteo on a steep incline. He climbed up the stairs into the blackness above, starting to breath heavily when the stairs maintained their slope over the next couple of minutes. The air began to get lighter and warmer as he ascended, causing his vision to elongate and blur on the edges. Luteo pushed harder, determined to prove himself and his fitness.

Luteo raised his foot for another step and almost spilled forward when his footing disappeared into thin air. Gasping air through his inflamed throat, Luteo stood at the top of the staircase and waited for his vision to return. A short hallway lay ahead of him, framed by a small doorway that opened the hallway up to a room beyond it. Luteo paced towards the end of the hallway, and almost forgot to breath as the doorway opened to a cavern of a similar size to the one he first entered. Instead of being circled by other doorways however, this cavern opened into thin air. The emptiness spread before him, with no floor to the cavern visible. Luteo could hear rushing rapids deep below, carrying a torrent of spring water deep into the mountainside.

Luteo turned his eyes upward and saw a thin rock bridge bisecting the thin air before him. He scoured the walls around him, trying to discern another pathway in the sheer rock that might provide a more stable route. Seeing nothing, he turned his eyes back to the stone bridge ahead.

The bridge was barely wide enough for each of his foot. He would have to place each foot ahead of the other, inching into the void ahead. Luteo closed his eyes and drew air into his lungs, summoning the courage to step out into the precipitous vacuum. Remembering the days of climbing the thin boughs of Berarbor, he imagined he was simply a small hop from a soft bed of grass with Pern egging him on from the safety below.

Luteo opened his eyes and stepped out onto the bridge. He kept his eyes forward as he inched along, fixated upon the end of the bridge as it disappeared into the dark grey of the cavern. He felt the updrafts of cool, humid air rushing up and around his balanced legs, rustling his fur and chilling his outstretched arms. Hours seemed to melt by as Luteo made his way forward, his focus trained entirely on his steps and his balance.

"Lu," echoed a small voice throughout the cavern, so quiet that Luteo wasn't even sure he really heard it. His ears pricked as he placed his foot down, but his attention was already broken. His left leg shot out ahead of him, knocking tiny pebbles and dust from the rough bridge edge. His balance shifted backwards, and Luteo fell, his left thigh catching the top of the bridge. Grabbing the stone bridge with both arms, he hugged with all his might to keep himself from twisting into the abyss.

Straining, but stable, Luteo awkwardly righted himself so that he straddled the walkway, hugging it with all his might. His heart was beating a thousand times a minute, his chest heaving with his rapid breathing. Luteo forced himself to imagine he was in his family's living room, bathing in the warmth cast from the small fireplace that crackled in the silence. As his breath and heart calmed, Luteo opened his eyes and pushed himself with great care back onto his feet. Forcing every other thought from his mind, Luteo fell back into his rhythm, placing one foot before the other.

Luteo was entranced in his pace when he noticed the lack of cool air rushing up around him. With great caution he raised his eyes from the small section of stone before him to see a rock wall materialize out of the black. He inched forward until his feet touched the cool stone floor before throwing himself forward onto the landing. Hugging the solid ground beneath him, Luteo wept and thanked Tarsus to feel the earth beneath his chest.

Luteo lay in the dirt and dust for a few more moments before summoning the strength to push himself back up to his feet and continue his trek into the darkness. Before him, another archway was carved into the solid stone wall. Luteo walked through the archway to find himself on a small balcony above an intricate web of lines below.

Squinting into the dark grey of the abyss below him, Luteo was able to make out a larger circular shape with thin geometric lines spreading out from the walkways. A single torch shined in the center of the circle, almost invisible from the gallery high above. Luteo turned in a circle and found stairs to his right which followed the edge of the wall, allowing him to approach the labyrinth from his perch. Starting down the stairway, Luteo kept his eyes trained on the maze below, trying to memorize the twisting and turning of the walls that led each pathway through the circle.

The air was thick and stagnant as Luteo took the final step onto the labyrinth's level. The walls obfuscated his view, leaving him to pull solely on his attempt at memorizing the pathways branching outward from his starting point. The stairway had ended in a small room with an open ceiling, leaving only one way into the labyrinth ahead. As Luteo made his way forward he tried his best to keep his bearings, remembering where the balcony high above had punctured the dome of stone around him.

Before Luteo had made five paces into the maze he was presented with a choice. A walkway turning left seemed to curve towards the center, while the walkway to his right angled outward to the maze walls. He paused a moment before turning to the left, hoping that any progress he made towards the center would place him closer to the exit.

Luteo continued onwards, making a right, then a right, followed by a left, until he was turned around and devoid of any sense of direction. Looking up at the ceiling above, Luteo noted that he was moving further away from the walls surrounding the labyrinth, suggesting that he was making his way closer to the exit in the center. As he reached another turn in the pathway and pivoted to his right, Luteo saw a small crumpled pile of cloth further down from his position. He paused for a moment, looking for any signs of movement. Seeing none, he took care to move without noise as he approached the pile. When he was only a few paces away, he was overcome by a rich and sweet smell lingering over the cloth before him. Bright splotches of red stained the wall above the pile of clothes. Unable to make out the form of the shape before him, Luteo approached further. A

STEVIE B. B. KING

sick sense of nausea and dread washed over his body as he began to pick out body parts in the pile before him.

The sallow cloak that lay before Luteo held the remains of a small Olympa. The blood was still sticky and reflective, suggesting that she had died within the last few hours. Luteo held his breath and surveyed the poor wreckage that had come of her body. Her light fur was matted and slick, her arm broken at a strange angle and folded under her body. Luteo wondered as to how she could have ended up like this when he turned his head on a swivel as the realization hit him—there was something hunting them in the maze.

Luteo froze and truly listened, as if for the first time. Rather than looking for spatial clues that would lead to the exit, Luteo was now realizing his life depended on being able to avoid whatever had encountered the Olympa that lay before him. Kneeling over her body, he placed his hands over her shoulder and muttered a brief blessing of Tarsus. Luteo knew he had no time to waste, as his best bet at getting out alive was getting out quick. Jumping to his feet, he continued at a brisk jog down the pathway ahead. Left, right, left, left, Luteo jogged forward and breathed with a steady pace.

A clicking sound echoed through the maze, bouncing off the walls behind him. Luteo turned and saw nothing, only the dead-end turn from which he had just run. The clicking started with a slow pace, then sped up as it increased in pitch. Luteo turned forward and continued his way, scanning the ceiling above to see if he was moving in the direction of the center of the chamber where the torch was located. He was unable to see the walls that had surrounded the labyrinth on all sides – a good sign that he was getting close.

The clicking died down but was replaced with a quiet scratching noise. Luteo kept his pace but turned his head over his shoulder. No movement in his periphery caught his eye. The scratching ebbed in and out, making it hard to pinpoint exactly where it was coming from. It sounded like the leaves high above Berarbor shaking in a deep summer wind, the dried twigs rustling and hustling all around him. Luteo turned another corner and was surprised to find he was staring at the torch that was mounted above a hole in the center of the labyrinth—he had found the exit.

Luteo bounded toward the center, but found his attention broken by the sudden deep vibrations coming from the hallway to his right. Luteo turned his head and saw the creature that occupied the maze. Tiny yellow eyes punctured the obscure background of its shaggy, black hair. The creature had too many legs, sticking out at odd angles from behind its ripe thorax; two glistening fangs hung drawn and dripping in the shimmering torch-light. The creature got to its feet as Luteo continued running to the circular hole in the middle of the labyrinth. Luteo recognized the scratching noise from earlier as he saw the thick, coarse hairs rubbing between the legs and body of the creature. He recognized the clicking noise as the creature flicked its fangs together, stimulating juices from its maw.

The terrible sight was too much for Luteo—he blocked his vision with his arm as he ran towards the exit in the ground. The fur on the back of his neck raised as he felt the creature moving closer, sensing his warmth and his anxiety. He was ten paces out, then five as he sprinted towards the torchlight. He glanced over and saw the creature bounding towards him, faster than he could ever hope to be. Luteo didn't know if he was going to make it. He fell towards the exit as the creature sailed through the air.

Luteo was thrown into darkness as he fell into the black hole beneath him. A deep screech echoed on the walls around him as the creature lamented his escape into the sections below. Luteo landed with a soft thump on a deep bed of moss that was growing beneath the light of the torch above. He jumped to his feet to survey the area around him, making sure that he wasn't falling from the frying pan above into the fire below. Nothing was moving; the empty chamber was devoid of anything that could harm Luteo.

He took a deep breath and sat back down on the moss. Holding his head in paws, Luteo gathered himself. He remembered Kermodei's warnings—many would enter but not all would leave. When he closed his eyes, he saw flashes of the broken Olympa body lying in cloaks, flashes of the hairy creature bounding toward him, flashes of the abyss opening before him as he lost his footing on the bridge. Isabell wreathed in light as she was swallowed by the flames.

Luteo forced himself back to his feet and calmed his breath. He wiped his cheeks to find moisture on his face, tears from the memories that resurfaced. He had to keep moving forward, and the only way to do so was to harden his resolve and pass this Trial. He turned in a slow circle, examining the small stone chamber that he found himself in. A small entryway was hewn into the rock wall at waist height. Luteo approached it, and clambered into the tunnel, crawling forward.

Luteo peered ahead and saw a small bright circle shining from the other end of the tunnel. He imagined it was the warm and clear air surrounding the Trial doorways they had first entered, where the dank and rot of this cavern could be forgotten in seconds. The circle grew as he inched his way forward, moving from a saucer to a dinner plate, swallowing the dark with each step. The tunnel changed its slope before Luteo could adjust, and he slid forward towards the bright hole in the wall.

Luteo shot out of the tunnel onto the dirt floor, bathed in the sunlight coming from above. He drew a deep sigh as he turned onto his back and gazed up at the sky above. The sun must have started setting, because the deep red of early morn had been replaced by a dark maroon.

"Took you long enough," a deep voice spat from his right. Luteo scrambled to his feet to find Titanus sitting in the dust against the wall opposite him. Behind Titanus was a smooth stone wall that shot upwards into the sky—the height of five Ursa. His eyes scanned the top of the wall, trying to find an edge in the solid line that meant his freedom from this Trial. Luteo turned in a complete circle, before turning back to Titanus. They were trapped with no way to climb out.

"I've been waiting for someone to show up. And now I can finally get out of here." Titanus pushed himself onto his feet. Luteo was taken aback by his size up close—he knew the Terrera was big from afar but standing before him he was practically Luteo's height and half again. "Do you see that engraving over on the far wall?" Titanus asked as he pointed to the wall opposite Luteo. Luteo stepped forward towards the engraving and read from the stone.

> *You find yourself in chasms deep,*
>
> *If you are alone you ought to weep,*
>
> *Luck would place your opponent here,*
>
> *If they don't show, you'll rot for years.*
>
> *We watch and wait and see you fight,*
>
> *Dominate your opponent or say goodnight.*

Before he could react, Luteo felt Titanus rushing towards him. He tried to turn to force Titanus across his back, but Titanus adjusted and grappled Luteo's arms as he pulled out of the way. Titanus flipped him over his thigh, causing Luteo to fall backwards into the dust and grime on the chamber floor.

"Don't you get it, cub-brain? I have to destroy you to get out of this trap," Titanus growled through his clenched jaw. He slashed downwards with his outstretched claws, drawing deep gashes into Luteo's outstretched forearm. Luteo howled in pain and kicked Titanus up and over his head, throwing him into the space behind Luteo.

"Destroy? Who said anything about destroy?" Luteo rolled to his feet with a panic in his voice, sensing that Titanus was reading the inscription with a darker interpretation.

"Didn't you hear Kermodei at the beginning of all this? It's kill or be killed, and my family doesn't have Ursa that let themselves be killed." Titanus sneered at Luteo as he rolled himself forward and began to circle Luteo. Luteo backed up against the cavern wall, looking past Titanus for an escape path of any kind.

"There's nowhere for you to run, weak one. Just face me like the Ursa you're trying to become. I will pretend like you didn't try to weasel your way out of this when I speak of my triumph," Titanus sneered in a sick voice. Luteo felt a wave of anger wash over his body. He gathered himself up and wiped the blood from his gash.

"Who said anything about running?" Luteo asked as he dove towards Titanus. Luteo's change of heart surprised Titanus, and he didn't react in time to stop Luteo from slashing his thigh. Titanus fell to his knee as Luteo ran but whipped around his other claw to catch Luteo's side as he passed. A thin spray of red spurted onto the dry floor as the two Ursa separated.

"You surprised me, little one," Titanus chuckled as he held his leg. "It won't happen again."

Luteolus ran at Titanus and faked a jab to his left. Titanus read him like a book and swatted down his counter-jab. Titanus turned in a roundhouse kick and hit Luteolus square in the chest. Luteo fell backwards, winded and struggling to sit up. Titanus didn't quit and kept forward with his offensive push. He ground his knee into Luteo's chest and placed his paw on Luteo's neck.

"Shush now. Just let yourself fall to sleep," Titanus whispered before he licked his lips. Luteo felt himself grabbing at the strings of reality, as the edges of his vision began to fade. The black was creeping in. Luteo felt a wave of panic and dread come over his body, yearning to see Isabell but not yet ready to go to the other side. The last bit of the tunnel in Luteo's vision was fading.

Luteo sank his claws into the dust lining the chamber floor and threw it upwards into Titanus' eyes. Luteo couldn't see, but felt as Titanus moved backwards, allowing Luteolus to push forward. Luteo couldn't give him time to recover. Blindly, he threw himself forward to where he thought Titanus' body would be. He felt his paws sink into fur and moved his paws up to reach Titanus' neck above his shoulders. Reversing their position, Luteo knelt on Titanus as he regained his vision. Specks, first, then splotches of Titanus laying in the dirt with Luteo's knee on his chest. Having learned from his own trick, Luteo pushed Titanus' arm behind his back, and pinned it to the ground.

Titanus gurgled as he struggled for air. Luteo wanted to keep pressing and pressing, but his sister's voice echoed inside his head. He couldn't kill another Ursa.

"Yield!" Luteo yelled at Titanus as he pushed down on his chest. "I will not kill you, but you must yield." Titanus replied with a defiant rasp as he tried to push Luteo off. Luteo doubled his strength and pushed down harder.

Titanus' eyes fought for a few more moments but lost their edge after Luteo gave no signs of easing up. In a second, the eyes were full of fear, pleading for respite. Luteo saw this and instantly removed the pressure, standing up over Titanus.

"I yield," Titanus coughed as he sucked in air.

At the exact same moment Titanus yielded, a deep vibration echoed throughout the chamber, as thick blocks of stone slid out from the wall. The blocks expanded in a spiral pattern, creating a staircase that circled the chamber and allowing them to escape upwards toward the sky.

Titanus sputtered and coughed on the ground, while Luteo waited. Once Titanus was quiet, Luteo stretched out a paw to pull him upwards. Titanus glared at Luteo and got to his feet on his own. He spit at Luteo's offer for assistance and began to climb the blocks up to the exit. Luteo sighed and followed suit.

Once they reached the top level of the chamber, Luteo could see other tunnels that sank into the ground, like the chamber from which they had just exited. Ursa were sitting and standing around the field, dazed after going through such an intense trial. Luteo scanned the horizon and saw Kermodei standing on a grassy mound a click away. He watched the slow accumulation of Ursa, noting those who had made their way through, and those who were absent from the somber celebration.

Kermodei turned and seemed to recognize Luteo. He waved, a slow arc of his cloaked arm, and then turned to continue his surveillance. Luteo felt a pang of anger and guilt deep in his gut. He remembered the broken shape of the Olympa in the labyrinth. He remembered the feeling of dread as Isabell welcomed him into the darkness. And he remembered fire and light and heat and losing Isabell.

Naka

Naka sat next to Kane and across from Shisuta in her offices on the second floor of the tavern. "So, let me make sure I understand correctly," Kane said. "You're Naka's aunt, and Naka's mother, your sister, ran away from her—your—family to marry Naka's dad?"

Shisuta laughed. "Yes, for the fourth time, you have that straight."

"How are we just hearing about this?" Kane asked, bewildered. "It's not just me, right? It seems like even Naka didn't know about this. Naka, you didn't know about this, right?"

"No, Kane, I did not know about this." Naka spat out. "He brings up a good point, though, Miss Hageshi—"

"—Please, call me Shisuta. Or aunty Shisuta, if you'd like."

"Shisuta, how is it that I did not know I had any family left on my mother's side? Why has my own family been kept a secret from me?"

Shisuta paused to collect herself before answering. "Your mother and I came from a proud Yamahito upbringing. We weren't nobles of the exalted sort that inherit land and titles, but our family did have wealth, and with wealth often comes pride. Your mother met your father right here in this city, when he came to sell some of the pearls he'd collected over a few years of diving. She chanced upon his makeshift pearl stand and they struck up a conversation. It was the kind of encounter you'd read about in a fairytale: a handsome man from a poor upbringing falls madly in love with a beautiful woman from a stable, higher class, and she with him. The real world, however, seldom mimics fantasy. Your father stayed in this city long after he had sold the last of his pearls and got a job working at the loading docks. Your parents saw each other in secret for several months before they came to my parents to plead that they be allowed to marry.

"My parents would not stand for their proposal. Our kind, Yamahito of a higher class, do not associate with lower peoples and they certainly do not marry them, they said. On top of that, my parents had already pledged your mother to a different man, an older Yamahito of a noble family that had long since lost any riches. The arranged marriage would grant our family an air of nobility and would grant his family wealth. A match made in aristocratic heaven. But your father and your mother had a different idea. They snuck off in the night, with some help from yours truly, and they traveled back to Manaolana to wed. There they stayed."

Naka tried his best to process all that she'd said. "But why, then," he started, "did I not even hear of you? Why did my father keep my aunt a secret from me, when he himself clearly had kept in contact with you?"

Shisuta sighed. "Your mother's departure brought embarrassment to our family. To save face, they offered my hand in marriage to her suitor in lieu of hers. The other family accepted, and a short time later I wed the man to whom your mother had been promised. I had filled the gap left by your mother's escape. I think your mother felt guilty that her departure turned her fate into mine. She did not contact me for years, and though I supported her marriage to your father, I hated her for her silence. It wasn't until she lay on her deathbed a few years later that I received a letter from her.

"I did visit her then, and I met you, though you were far too young to remember our encounter. I talked with your father at length during that trip and met your obachan too. It was then that I first heard his plans of revolution, and it was that same stay that I became convinced to support his efforts. After that meeting, the sensitive nature of what your father and I discussed from then on precluded any extra trips to your village that would have raised suspicion. I could not see you and visit you because the act would have attracted too much attention, especially from my parents and my husband's family, who you have to remember are still very well connected politically. After that meeting we mainly kept in contact through trusted messengers, aside from your father's occasional trips to the city. But my visiting Manaolana was off the table."

Naka sat back. "I—I don't know what to say." He looked down at the floor for a moment, then back up at Shisuta. "I suppose I should first say thank you. I've learned more details about my father and my mother's life together than he has told me in eighteen years of my life."

"Your father still weeps for the loss of your mother, Naka. Remember that. He had planned to tell you, but he did not find the strength to do so before the red sun."

"And there it is. The red sun." Naka nodded. "I suppose now's as good a time as any to get back into what brought us here. After the red sun happened, my father started his revolution and sent me here, to you. Why? What do you have for me? My father mentioned that you'd have another task for us."

"And I do," Shisuta smiled. She rose from her seat and opened a cabinet next to her desk, taking out a long object wrapped in brown cloth. "Naka Pikala," she said, handing the item to him. "This belongs to you."

Naka unwrapped the cloth and discovered a long, ornate sword. It was of the same kind that both the guards in Kalani and Boto's henchmen wore, though he could somehow tell that this particular sword had been crafted of much higher quality. It shined even in the dimly lit room, and its edge seemed to disappear into a single point of sharpness. He turned it over carefully in his hands and saw a symbol on the left side of its hilt. Stamped onto the leather handle sat a red half-sun, rising as if to meet the metal blade. He looked up at his aunt.

"Is this the same sun—"

"—The same sun you saw not long ago in Manaolana. Yes, it is. We saw it here too. In fact, the whole of Godsdorf saw that sun. You two are on a very important mission. And you're going to need this sword."

"Excuse me," Kane said, "but one thing I don't understand is why you would want to help a Nakai uprising, what with your extensive ties to the Yamahito people here." He added quickly, "no offense."

"My dear Kane. Did you think that only the Nakai stood to gain from disrupting Empress Karuto's rule? There are Yamahito that also stand to benefit. Don't think that the Yamahito present a united front. There are ripples on the surface, and riptides beneath. "As for me," she said, "you could also say it's a bit personal."

"Now," she continued, "there are some things I need to tell you about where you're going and what to expect. You're heading to a mountain east of here. Mount Vesus. You're to meet up with two other groups much like yourselves. Have you heard of the Corvideans and the Ursa?"

Naka sat back in his chair and exchanged a puzzled glance with Kane. "You mean the bird-people and bears that used to roam the land back when the gods first created Godsdorf?"

"Oh, boy," Shisuta said. "Nephew, I think it's time we had a chat about the birds and the bears."

Raban

As they approached the fields of Chasteria, the bald warrior declared that they needed absolute silence until they reached the city's gate and, until then, their rhinos needed to walk in a single-file line. Raban tried his best to follow these orders, while also trying to not slip off the boney back of his rhino. It was not as easy as he hoped. Raban's rhino seemed to be the smallest and most rambunctious of all the rhinos. The little beast had nearly bucked Raban off multiple times in the woods, but after his earlier embarrassment, Raban refused to let go of the ropes. He kept his head up and scanned the horizon as he bounced up and down.

Raban was amazed by the never-ending fields of bizarre plants, dotted with small wooden nests, and was fascinated that these nests were not in trees. They sat on the groundfloor as squat singular structures built out of dead trees. These nests and Inlanders' fields stretched out for as far as the eye could see. Raban shivered. There was no doubt that the Inlanders must outnumber the Arborns more than 10 to 1. This fact was startling when Raban considered the fact that the Lord Mayor always spoke about their great odds of winning in battle against the Inlanders. She must believe that the Huginn warriors were something quite exceptional or else she was stretching the truth quite far.

After what felt like the entire night, the rhinoback warriors in front of Raban stopped. They had reached the city gates of Chasteria! The walls of the city were even higher than Raban imagined, nearly as tall as a full-grown Thuma tree. The walls were built out of boulders like the ones that Raban had seen once near the Forest Edge. At each corner, massive tree-like structures stood apart from the rest of the wall, stabbing into the air with gold flags waving above them. Behind these stone defenses, there lay one stone building after another, almost as numerous as the small wood huts outside in the fields. In the center of these giant buildings rested one massive, dark-domed building with four piercing guard towers protecting it. Its steep dome shadowed everything else in the twilight. If they cut all the trees down in Arbornesta, Raban wasn't sure they could build as gigantic a building. The magnitude of his mission started to weigh on him.

"I wonder where Lord Chasta lives?" Mudskap quipped from behind Raban.

"I wonder...and I think Muni is somewhere up it. I don't feel too confident about this plan right now," responded Raban in a monotone voice.

From up ahead, Raban heard some discussion. He had fallen behind a bit and kicked his rhino softly to catch up.

"After my signal, like I said, we all charge. My rhino should be able to knock a hole in the front gate with its horns, and then most of you will go with the youngling to the Lord's house. I want Junji to lead that attack. According to our sources, Muni should be in the dungeon of the East Tower, that kraven king's favorite little playpen. Once you get there, find the girl and bring her back to the gate. I will lead the rest of us to that kraven's family house. We will find his niece, snag and bag her, and bring her back here. We need to do this quick. The alarm will raise right after I hit the gate. Any questions?"

"Last one back has got personal Vali duty for a week straight. Does that sound like a fair deal, Wuden?" said Junji with a small laugh from her cracked beak. Raban noticed the scar that crossed up over her beak and across one of her eyes, which was completely white.

"You got it, but let's make the stakes a bit higher. Two weeks. And Huginn better save the last soul who is stuck with this duty," laughed the bald one, Wuden, without a trace of fear in his voice.

"You've got a deal!" said Junji, and she looked right at Raban. Her white eye and dark black one pierced through him. "Hey, don't make me late, youngling. I'm not going to lose this bet because of you. I will leave you and your stupid little sister if you take too long. Follow me through the gate and stay close, okay?"

Raban's throat could not squeeze out a sound, his beak felt too dry. He could only nod.

"Alright that covers it, no more time to waste. Here we go! Everyone ready?" cried the bald leader. The other warriors knocked hard on their shields.

Wuden smiled, and he kicked into his rhino, charging the wooden gate. All the other warriors screamed "For Huginn!" and chased behind their leader. His wide-horned rhino crashed through the front gate, splintering shards of wood everywhere. Raban tried his best to follow his guide, Junji, as she flew towards the East Tower.

They only ran into a handful of guards on the way, all of which Junji skillfully handled with her rhino. She almost appeared to be toying with the last one, as her rhino gored it multiple times with each horn. His blood splattered over her scarred face, leaving her looking deranged.

When they finally reached their destined tower, they all hopped off, and one of the heavier warriors kicked down the door. Raban made sure to grab his pack and his polespear off his rhino as they ran into the tower. The steps ran both ways, but Junji, without hesitation, led them towards the basement. After only a few feet down, the stench of the dungeons soaked into everyone's beaks. The air was heavy and filled his mouth with a warm taste of rotting Slange meat. He almost vomited halfway down the steps, but they continued going deeper and deeper. They passed empty cells, some with decaying bodies, but there was no sign of his sister. On the final flight of steps, however, Raban could hear crying, and instantly recognized Muni's wail.

He swung down the steps as fast as he could, pushing passed Junji. In the final cell, on a blood-stained cot, lay his sister. She was tied to the metal posts of the bed, and her small round face was covered in blood.

"It's me, Muni! I'm here, just hold on!" Raban called as he slammed against her iron cell door.

"Rabe?" Muni said, her voice shaking.

"Yes, it's me, Muni! I've brought help." He looked over at Junji, who was working on the lock with some keys she nabbed on the way.

"And here you go, we are making record time and let's keep it that way," Junji said as she pulled open the iron gate.

"Muni!" Raban cried as he ran and cut the ropes from her hands with his polespear. "I'm so sorry."

Muni tried to open her beak for a smile, but she was too exhausted. He could tell from her eyes that she was overwhelmed with relief.

"What have they done to you? Has Lord Chasta or any of the guards done anything to you?"

Her face turned sour. The life in her eyes went a bit duller, and she shook her head.

"It's fine, Rabe. It's all better now that you are here," she said with a soft whimper. Her eyes would not leave Raban's.

"Is this family reunion almost over because we need to go!" screamed Junji, standing next to the other warriors at the gate. Raban did not have time to process everything, but he pulled his sister up.

"Can you walk?" he asked.

She nodded.

"When the moment comes, follow my lead, okay?" Raban whispered before they left the cell.

She looked confused, but she nodded again.

They started to follow Junji and company up the steps. It was slow, but Muni was regaining her strength with every step. Her soft feathers were painted red and matted against her body, yet her body pulsed with energy. When they reached the top of the steps, the warriors filed out and Junji waited for them at the door.

Instead of stepping outside with them, Raban turned and shoved Junji as hard as he could and yelled. "Run up, Muni!"

She took off without hesitation, running up the winding steps of the tower. Raban was right behind her, running as fast as he could with his pack and polespear. Junji had tumbled down, but Raban could hear her regrouping fast.

"We've got ourselves a runner, boys! Spread out around the tower in case they glide down. I will follow them up, don't forget, we are not losing this bet!"

Junji's heavy talons scratched the stone floor as she jumped from step to step behind them.

Raban burst into the guard's room on the top floor, with Muni in his arms. She had fallen into a heap on the last few steps. He could still feel her heart pounding from the run, and her beak was very dry; she needed water. There was a hooded figure waiting there, and two guards lying unconscious on the straw-covered floor.

"Ah, the Chosen One has arrived, and sounds like with some unwanted company," said the hooded figure as he stepped forward from the shadows. The sounds of Junji's talons were not far down the steps.

"Yes, we have no time, she is on our wings! What's the next step?" Raban demanded.

"Of course, I set up this rope that connects to the base of a tree outside of Chasteria, and from this height, all you need to do is climb on the rope and take it to freedom. There will be two rhinos waiting for you to ride. Take them and follow where the Sun rises. The journey is only a few days from here. Just follow, and I know you will be fine."

"Oh, for Huginn's sake, and how am I going to climb that with this pack, my sister, and my polespear?" asked Raban, with little patience.

"I have rope. Hold still." The hooded figure grabbed a pile of cut rope and tied his sister to his chest and around his pack as fast and tight as he could. "Maybe try using that talon you've got to ride down the rope?"

"That's your plan?" Raban said as Junji slammed into the room.

"Oh my, oh my! Lord Mayor isn't going to be happy when she hears that the Chosen One betrayed his own people to help these filthy Inlanders."

She swung her short dagger towards Raban. His mobility was limited by the ropes and tripped over the weight as he moved away. She caught him with blade under his left wing. He fell forward to the windowsill where the shadow figure caught him and his sister. Then this unknown friend stepped forward, drawing out a large broadsword and cracking the blade against Junji's next dagger swipe.

"Great meeting you, Chosen one, but I think it's time for you to go!" squawked the cloaked figure as he grappled with Junji.

"Don't even try gliding out of here, youngling. I've got the entire city covered in warriors. You won't survive the fall." Junji wheezed as the cloak figure pushed her against the wall.

Raban put his talon over the hanging rope. His sister was dangling from his body but was tied securely.

With one deep breath, Raban pushed off the stone windowsill and gripped tight to the talon with both hands. The talon's hooked edge held the rope perfectly, and they slid down towards freedom. His wings ached under the weight of Muni and his pack. He could hear the city alarm had been sounded. Torches along the city walls were being lit.

"Hey, there's the boy!"

"Wait, is he flying?"

"Somebody catch him!" screamed familiar voices from below.

There was panic below them as they flew. Raban clutched the talon with new-found strength. He was determined to not let Muni be taken again. They flew high over the wall on the rope, landing at the base of an old thuma tree outside of the city. As the cloaked figure claimed, there were two large rhinos tethered to the tree, waiting for them.

Raban placed Muni and his pack on one. He nudged the pack hard a few times.

"Hey, I'm sleeping in here!" called out Mudskap in pain.

"Alright, friend, time to start pulling your weight on this adventure. My sister is in some serious pain and not doing well. Can you help her?" asked Raban. Sweat was beading on his forehead. His left wing was bleeding.

Mudskap pushed his squishy, brown, spotted body out of the pack. He looked at Raban and Muni, who was going in and out of sleep.

"Oh, I see. You two aren't looking like the healthiest birds I've ever seen. I'll see what I can do."

After a few moments, Muni's wounds were cleaned, and her eyes were coming back to life.

"Rabe…"

"Yes, Muni! What is it?"

"I knew you would come back for me. Thank you."

Raban swallowed her little body with his wings and gave her a careful hug. His eyes were burning.

He looked down and her eyes were dripping. She was smiling through the tears.

"Well are you ready to ride? We need to reach a lake in a few days, I'll explain why as we go. The journey should not take more than a few days. Also, Great Auntie gave us some snacks, he pulled out the small bag that she had hid in his pack. It was full of dried Slange meat and two hand-woven water jugs. We should be alright. Do you feel ready?"

"As always, Rabe. Here we go!" she said with a smile and grabbed a water jug and a handful of the Slange meat.

Raban showed her the proper way to hop onto a rhino's back. Riding through the forest, they chatted through the night, swapping tales about their mother and father. For a while, it felt like nothing had changed between them.

Over the course of the next few nights, Muni explained the odd and cruel treatment she received from the Inlanders. Some were quite nice to her and asked her about life back in the trees. They seemed genuinely curious. However, Lord Chasta and his noble friends enjoyed playing games such as who could pluck the most feathers out before she screamed, or who could dig their talon deeper into her back before she bled. Every night, they would play some form of "noble" game with Muni.

As she released these memories, Muni's smile returned. Every story she shared, she shed some horrible memory from her time there. She rode faster and played more as they continued to wind through the hills leading to Mt. Vesus. One night, they sat around a fire and read from their mother's Huginn Holy Book. He read from a chapter that discussed the battle between light and dark in the shadow of Mt. Vesus. According to Huginn, this land was cursed and should never be explored except by careful and prudent monks. Yet when Muni and Raban read this section, there was no fear in their eyes when they looked at each other. Instead, they just laughed. The next morning, as they rode over other densely forested hills, they saw the most beautiful lake that either of them had ever seen. They had made it.

Luteo

Luteo lay on his cot in the tent just on the outskirts of the Liberalia grounds and was mulling over the scarring events of the day, when Kermodei announced his arrival. Using his cloaked arm to push aside the draped tent door, Kermodei cleared his throat and waited expectantly. Pern and Erem were both lying in their cots but took this as a signal to leave the tent for a few moments. They jumped to their feet, bowing as they passed Kermodei and exited the tent.

Luteo seemed not to register Kermodei's entrance and didn't acknowledge it when Kermodei sat at the foot of Luteo's bed.

"Luteo, I need to share something with you," Kermodei spoke in a soft whisper. Luteo continued to keep his eyes closed, ignoring Kermodei's statement. "It has to do with your sister." At this sentence, Luteo's eyes burst open in a mixed look of anger and curiosity.

"Do you have any idea what the red sun we saw today means?" Kermodei questioned as he placed his hand on Luteo's bandaged leg.

"What does this have to do with my sister?" Luteo spat. He rolled over onto his side. "Don't use my sister as a toy in your games, Kermodei."

"I do not ask to be cruel, Master Luteolus." Kermodei drew his hand back. "The red sun today means much more than you might think. In fact, I have a suspicion that the assassination attempt on Denmaster Bern was no accident." Luteo sat up straight in bed, wincing as he strained his arm and leg.

"What are you talking about? It sounds like you're saying someone had planned to kill Isabell."

"I'm not entirely sure," Kermodei said in a slow pace as he mused over his thoughts. "But when I saw the crimson sun today as the Liberalia began this morning, I knew that it had to be more than fate considering our timing." Kermodei pulled a small bundle of tied cloth from the depths of his cloak. He placed the package on the bed in front of Luteo and looked up at him.

"What is this, Master Kermodei?" Luteo asked, gesturing at the bundle.

"I am going to give you your own Trials, Luteo. The sun this morning was a symbol that the time has come for a great change." Kermodei paused and stared at the package between them.

"Listen to me carefully, Luteo. I am sending you to the West, over the mountains of the Ursolympa and into the valley below. There, you will find a sole mountain that stands against the horizon like a thorn in the side of Godsdorf. This mountain spits the very fire of Tarsus on the earth and can be a dangerous place. On the northern side of this mountain, is a lake nestled between two valleys. You must arrive at this lake in exactly seven days' time."

Luteo waited for Kermodei to continue speaking but found him silent.

"What does this have to do with Isabell? All I want to do is get back to my family in Berarbor, to be able to mourn her properly and send her to Tarsus," Luteo swore in anger, expecting Kermodei to impart more wisdom.

"Be calm, young one. I understand this time is excruciating for you. Do you remember what I told you the night before the Liberalia? How if we could remember the sins and wounds of our forefathers, that we would solve all of life's pains?" Kermodei questioned Luteo.

Luteo nodded without speaking.

"How many before you do you think have lost so much more than you, for so much less? Isabell is everything to you, I understand that. But I need you to think past yourself for a moment. Can you save Isabell now? She is gone from us. Can you save the next Isabell? The next Ursa who is killed during a raid? Their father who will be killed if we fall into civil war?" Kermodei's breath was heaving as he tried to calm himself.

"The beginning of your story is already written Luteo. But you can compose the ending."

Luteo looked down at the bundle before him and placed his paws on it. He untied the knot on the top and unfurled the maroon cloak over his lap. The cloak was around his size and would fit the average Ursa in both height and width. Luteo was shocked to see an emblem sewn onto the cloak. A large crimson sun in the act of rising was placed on the middle of the cloak, with rays shining upward and outward. Luteo's jaw dropped, and he looked at Kermodei.

"Is... Is this the same sun as this morning?" Luteo asked.

"This cloak was given to me by my own Master, Master Crowtheri." Kermodei spoke as he stroked the sun on the back of the cloak. "Unlike you, I was given this cloak to safeguard it, to give it to the one who needed it when the time was right."

Kermodei paused, and then grabbed the cloak and placed it in Luteo's arms.

"The time is right. This cloak will protect you from any sharp weapon with the intent to maim, injure, or disfigure." Luteo scoffed in disbelief and grabbed a small dagger from his nightstand. He placed the tip of the dagger on the edge of the cloak and tried to slice through the cloak. To his surprise, the dagger slid over the cloak, stopping the blade from piercing the fabric. Luteo tried again, this time in the center of the cloak as it lay flat on his cot. Again, he found the blade slip out from his grip, and the cloak lay whole before him. Kermodei rose to his feet and gathered his robes around him.

"Pern, Erem, you may enter," Kermodei said. The tent was silent, and then Pern and Erem walked into the tent, heads hung in shame.

"I do not fault you for eavesdropping. In fact, it makes our lives easier, so we don't have to go through everything again. You will be joining Luteo on this Trial."

Pern grinned while Erem straightened in shock, before scratching his head.

"Master Kermodei, we cannot leave the Liberalia before it is completed. Otherwise we will return to our Kingdens in shame," Erem said to Kermodei, expecting his explanation to remind Kermodei why they couldn't leave the Liberalia prematurely.

"This is much larger than the Liberalia. What you do in a week will affect everyone in this land, regardless of race or home. I use all my power to grant you the honor of completing the Liberalia, despite your early departure. In fact, the completion of your Trials to come will mean much more than completing the Liberalia ever could," Kermodei explained.

Erem stood in silence, blinking slowly. Pern on the other hand, elbowed Luteo in the side and cried, "Alright then! When do we leave?"

"Tomorrow morning. Gather your supplies and leave before the sun rises." Kermodei moved toward the tent door and paused before he looked back towards Luteo.

"Good luck, Master Luteolus. I hope to see you return."

***

Luteo shook Pern awake an hour before the sunrise. Erem had already woken on his own and was collecting his belongings in a rucksack. His pickstaff was sheathed and laying on his cot, ready to be strapped to his back. The Ursa prepared for their departure in silence, rubbing the sleep from their eyes while wondering if they truly were about to embark on a journey over the mountains, leaving behind their childhood companions and venturing into new lands. Once they were ready to go, they stood in an awkward huddle near the front of the tent, not wanting to be the first or last to leave. Luteo took a deep breath and used his staff to push open the tent door. He paused and looked back at Erem and Pern.

"You two don't have to come with me, you know. I have no idea what we're getting into, and it's my sister who was hurt by this. I won't fault you if you want to stay."

"Oh, I'm coming with you brother. I've been by your side since we could speak back in Berarbor—how could I leave you when you need my help the most?" Pern puffed his chest out in a show of bravado, then pointed at Erem. "I can't speak for this cub-brain over here."

"I know we just met, Luteolus, but I do not take a personal Trial from Kermodei lightly. He would not send us from the Liberalia unless this is of the utmost paramount," Erem spoke in a slow voice, as he reasoned through his logic. Luteo smiled and nodded, before hoisting his pack higher on his shoulders. He turned back to the tent flap, and the three walked in single file outside of the tent.

***

The three Ursa walked in single file out of the Liberalia grounds and into the dense forest cover a few clicks away. They followed the path towards Ursolympa, Erem's home, which was nestled high in the mountains above and responsible for the exports of stone and minerals to the rest of the Kingdens. As the sun began to peak above the horizon to the East, Luteo and his companions turned and watched the first few rays illuminate the Liberalia amphitheater. The sun had returned to its normal color, the crimson shade of yesterday gone from its radiant surface. The surrounding valley looked much less threatening in the usual sunlight, the birds in the trees around them singing in chorus.

The Ursa returned to the trail and entered the darkness of the forest. It was not until late afternoon that their party popped out above the thinning tree-line, much higher in elevation and sweating through their cloaks. They paused for lunch and ate some of the provisions they had stowed in their packs, before pushing further on their journey.

That night, Luteo, Pern, and Erem camped in a small cave near the trail they had been following. Building a small fire so as to not draw attention, they fell asleep bundled in their travel cloaks. Rising before the sun the next morning, they donned their packs and continued traveling in the early sunlight. They passed the time by singing each other songs, Erem sharing the mining hymns of the Olympa while Pern and Luteo sang duets from Berarbor. Luteo shared tales of the spring feasts that his mother would put on as the snow thawed, while Pern would tell of his father berating him for finishing the last of candied acorns from their larder.

Two days later, Pern took the first step onto the thin ridge that split the mountain range from north to south, taking them from the land of the Ursa and into the land beyond. The three Ursa stood and drank in the view that most Ursa would never see in their lives. To the northwest, a large body of water spread inland, feeding the fertile pine forests that blanketed the rolling hills. To the southwest, a sole mountain stood alone against the horizon. Luteo pointed at the mountain with his staff.

"We have many clicks to travel yet, friends. We have four days to reach the base of the mountain that spits flame, and who knows how much longer we will need to be there after we arrive." Luteo readjusted the cloak around his shoulders to deaden the chill breeze that whipped across the peaks. Pern looked back in a cheeky grin.

"Then what are we waiting for?"

Naka

"Do you think what your aunt said was true?" Kane asked. "I mean, about the bird people and the bear people?"

"She called them Corvideans and Ursa, I think," Naka replied. "It seems crazy, but I don't have any reason to doubt what she's said so far. She knew many details of my father and his life."

"But, half-human, half-bird hybrids? That's nuts."

"I don't know, Kane. Is it so weird that two beings of different backgrounds, cultures, and appearances could fall in love? Maybe that's not so different than how my parents met and had me."

Kane looked at his feet, thinking of what to say next. "Sure. But it's not like with your parents, Naka. We've known Nakai and Yamahito our whole lives. We're all still human. Have you ever seen a Corvaydeean? An Orsa?"

"Corvidean and Ursa," Naka corrected. "But you have a point. Honestly, I don't know what to think any more."

The two of them walked through the streets, which were thankfully full of Nakai people in this part of the city. Shisuta had given them an address at which they could find Waiwai, and she had arranged transportation for them to leave town the following morning. They followed the directions she had written down for them and found themselves at the foot of an enormous building, of proportions that before this they had never seen. It rose five stories above the ground, sat behind a cast-iron fence, and had guards posted at every corner of the building. As they approached the guardhouse, the men at watch placed their hands over the hilts of their swords, as if to beg them to start something.

"Excuse me, sirs," Naka said. "We're here to visit with Waiwai Kamoi."

One of the guards chuckled. "I doubt that's true. What do you really want? Another pair of beggars to ask for scraps at the master's table?"

"Okay," Kane said. "We didn't want to have to pull this card. But we've come on the request of Lady Shisuta Hageshi, and if you don't open this gate for us we will have to tell her who exactly stopped us doing as she asked."

The guards quickly opened the gate. Naka and Kane walked up the long path to the main courtyard, which housed more groomed plants than either of them had ever seen in their lives. They passed two Zen gardens, each overseen by a robed man with a polished bald head. At the top of the dozens of steps leading up to the main villa, two more guards halted their advance. After explaining what they had just explained to the previous set of guards, they passed through the entrance and into an inner garden, which was somehow even more meticulously groomed than the one before.

They waited in two highly comfortable chairs in a spacious entry way for little over an hour when an attendant, no older than they, came out to greet them. "My master would like to apologize for the wait," the servant said.

"Wait—your master?" Naka asked. "But you're Yamahito. I thought Waiwai was a Nakai."

The woman bristled. "Waiwai Kamoi is indeed Nakai. The richest of all Nakai, in fact. I do indeed work for him, and yes, I am Yamahito. Is there a problem?"

"Oh, no, not at all." Kane pleaded. "Forgive my friend. We come from a place where Nakai do not have the same power that Waiwai wields. Let's start over. My name is Kane. My simple friend here goes by Naka. And you?"

The woman eyed Kane carefully, as if she suspected him of something. "My name is Sumato. Nice to meet you."

"Sumato, forgive me my comments," Naka said. "I did not mean anything more than surprise, and the fact that I was even surprised shows my ignorance. We are here to see Waiwai. Is Mr. Kamoi ready for us?"

"He is. And you're excused."

Sumato led the two villagers into the heart of the compound and to a room well-lit by many scented candles. Naka noticed more distinct scents than he could count, and yet he had to admit that all the scents went together perfectly, no doubt curated for this very experience. Sumato left them for a moment, and came back with a large man in tow, who wore a rich silk robe and a diamond encrusted cap.

"Hello, boys," said the large man. "My name is Waiwai Kamoi, richest of all Nakai." He let out a large, bellowing laugh. "At least that's what my number-crunchers tell me. Here, have some tea." He gestured to the teacups that Sumato had just placed in front of him. "What business do you have with me?"

"Mr. Kamoi," Naka started. "We're here on behalf of our parents, who to be blunt about it have started a rebellion of sorts in our village, Manaolana."

Waiwai's eyes opened wide for a brief second before he nodded deeply. "I see. I have heard of their rebellion in Manaolana. And, I assume, you would like me to support your cause?"

"Well, yes, sir. You've obviously done well for yourself here even under the rules of a Yamahito-biased society. There's no denying that. But as a Nakai man, surely you still feel the oppressive thumb of this Magatta government? With everything you've accomplished so far, I can only imagine what heights you could reach within a society that prizes your culture and background, rather than punishes it."

"You feel that even I have been shortchanged by this society? Look around, my dear. I have a compound larger than the town I grew up in. Noble families of Yamahito blood come to me and ask for my advice, for my resources. Have I not made it?"

"You have," Kane added. "But look back on your journey to this point. I do not know your story. But can it not be said that you surpassed barriers along the way that no Yamahito born would have had to cross? Where is the fairness in that? For every Nakai as gifted as you, there are a thousand Nakai who could be at least overseers, or landowners, or magistrates. Do they not deserve the same chance as a Yamahito born? Did you, as a young child, not deserve the same chances as one born into the right family?"

Waiwai stroked his manicured beard. "Of course, you raise a good point. When I look back on my life, I see many moments where my Nakai blood held me back or stunted my growth. And still I grew." He smiled. "I would be happy to support your parent's endeavors. Perhaps with time that movement can grow to encompass all of Sokoku, and one day every Nakai child can have the chance to prosper as I have. What do you need from me?"

Naka and Kane sat up in their chairs. "For now, sir, only your word that you'll help," Naka said. "We have another task that we must carry out, but after that we shall send word back to our village and our parents will surely have an ask or two of you."

"Then it is done. Sumato, please see these fine young men to the courtyard."

Sumato led them to the groomed grounds outside but stopped them as they turned to leave. "Excuse me," she said. "But what is the task that you must now accomplish? Forgive me for overhearing, but I can't imagine what would be more important than sending word of Mr. Kamoi's assistance back to your village."

"I'm afraid we cannot say," said Kane. "We have some business to attend to in the East, that's all."

Naka jabbed Kane in the ribs. "It's only straightforward trading. We're to sell some goods east of here and take the proceeds back to our parents."

"I see," Sumato said. "In that case, I will come with you."

"I'm sorry, what?" Naka asked.

"I am going to come with you on your journey."

Kane laughed. "That's not within your power to say. We're on our own mission. You can't just join us."

"And why not?" Sumato asked. "I know far more about this part of the country than you two do. Let me guess—this is your first trip outside of your village, no?"

Naka and Kane looked at each other and did not answer.

"That's what I thought. I've been to every major city in Sokoku and I've gone as far east as Komeiji. I can help you."

"And why would you want to?" Naka asked. "No offense, but you're Yamahito. Why would you want to support a rebellion against your own kind?"

"I may be Yamahito, but that does not mean my life is bliss. I still serve those far wealthier or nobler, and I still do not have land nor wealth nor a family name to claim. I have reason to dislike my lot under this empire just as you do."

Kane pulled Naka aside. "Remember what your aunt said, Naka. I think Sumato may be telling the truth."

Naka nodded. He turned to Sumato. "What of your work with Waiwai? We just made an alliance with him. We do not want to immediately tarnish that alliance by stealing one of his servants."

"I work for Waiwai on a conditional arrangement. When he first asked me to join his staff, I told him that I tend to roam, and as a roamer I reserve the right to leave my post whenever I please as long as I give him a day's notice, which I shall give to him tonight if you agree to let me come along with you. It's an unusual working arrangement, but I'm just that persuasive."

Kane smiled. "I'm beginning to see that. Come on, then. Meet us at our inn tomorrow morning, and we'll head for our destination just after breakfast. It's only a day or two from here."

The Chosen I

In the shadow of Mount Vesus, the impact of their journey began to weigh on Raban. As he watched Muni and Mudskap frolic in the blue glacial lake, he felt the scars on his body; the bump on his head from the Inlander guards, the small bite marks on his chest from the ants, and the deep cut in his inner wing from Junji. Since leaving his home many moons ago, Raban felt like he had lived many lives, all weaved together like his family home. As he watched Muni laughing and diving after Mudskap in the water, all his troubles felt so distant. He and his sister somehow made it here, alive, at a pristine lake in the shadow of a giant volcano with a new magical frog friend on a critical mission for some Resistance group he didn't even know existed a week ago. Raban couldn't help but laugh; it was all too wonderful and ridiculous.

Despite this light reprieve, he wondered who they were supposed to meet at this lake, and why nobody else was here yet. Raban put his pack and polespear next to a small red boulder by the lake and started to climb up one of the nearby oak trees to get a better view of the surrounding area. The trunk bark was much softer and easier to climb with his talons than the thuma trees of his forest, and he ascended to the top with ease. When he reached the canopy, he peered down below from a sturdy branch and watched Mudskap hopping after Muni around the lake as he spit water at her.

Not too far away from Muni in the reeds alongside the lake, Raban noticed some rustling. It was much stronger than the wind, and the movement was heading right towards Muni. The size and dark color of the creature was oddly familiar. It looked like another Giant River Otter!

Raban gulped hard and thought, *Oh for Huginn's sake not again.*

Without hesitation, Raban pulled the sharp talon necklace from his neck and swooped down from the tree, gliding on his wings right towards the thicket of reeds. As he landed only a few body lengths away, he gathered himself up and prepared for the worst.

"Muni get back! Ka'kaw, we have company!" Raban screamed, and glanced back towards Muni and Mudskap, who froze their play and stared at him.

"Whoever is in the reeds, identify yourself!"

Out from the dense reeds, crashed a massive brown bear, and jumped towards Raban with its massive chestnut paws swinging towards him. Raban ducked below the paws and swung the sharp talon at his attacker's legs, slashing deep across one of them. The bear fell to its knees, grabbing its injured limb with a sharp cry. From behind, two more large bears came out growling from the reeds and moving forward to protect their wounded comrade. Raban stepped back and checked on Muni and Mudskap. They were holding small rocks, also ready for battle.

"What have you done? We meant you no harm!" cried one of the darker bears without looking up from his friend.

"Then why were you sneaking up on us?" responded Raban, with the talon clenched tight in his right hand.

"What are you talking about? We were supposed to come to this lake, and we didn't expect others to be here, so we didn't know we were sneaking up on anyone!" the bear called as he held his friend's gashed leg.

The sudden realization that these folks might be part of the Resistance dawned on Raban. He lowered his talon.

"Wait, you were told to come here too?" Raban asked, his voice wavering.

"Yes, we were sent on a mission to come to this lake. We had no idea what to expect, but it was clear that we had to come to this specific lake after the red sun revealed itself in the sky," responded the other bear, wearing a heavy loose cloak.

"Well that's very curious because my Great Auntie told me the same thing after the red sun appeared too, and she also told me that others might be coming too. I just never expected them to look like you." Raban said, looking the bears up and down. He had never seen an Ursa before, only heard myths and legends of their type.

"Well, a curious situation we find ourselves in—now that I think about it, the only creature that I've ever seen like you attacked my people and killed my beautiful sister," responded the cloaked bear. His eyes flashed with anger as he pushed himself off the ground and started to head towards Raban.

Raban clenched his talon tight in his hand and raised it towards the bear.

"Stay back! I don't know what you are talking about, but we had nothing to do with that!"

The cloaked bear stopped just a few steps away.

"You damned bird things, you attacked my kingden and killed my sister, and now you try to attack me and my friends. I should have known something was awry," responded the bear, eyeing Raban's weapon carefully.

"Seriously, stay back!" Raban said as he swung the talon towards the bear.

Without hesitation, the bear stepped towards Raban and grabbed his arm.

"What is that symbol on the edge of your talon there?" asked the bear.

"Wait, what?" Raban startled, glanced down at the talon and saw the red sun markings on his family heirloom. "Oh that... yes it's a marking of the Resistance of my people," he said, stepping back in a defensive pose.

Without saying anything, the cloaked bear stepped back and turned around, exposing his back to Raban, and stitched into the backside of his cloak was the exact same red sun outline.

Muni gasped from behind.

"Well, we really do find ourselves in a very curious situation," said Mudskap as he hopped closer to the cloaked bear.

"Oh, and what might you be?" Asked one of the bears.

"Just the comic relief, from you blood-seeking imbeciles.... If you don't mind, I would like to help your friend out over here," Mudskap remarked as he hopped onto the leg of the wounded bear. Without asking, Mudskap started to work his magic, cleaning the gash and helping it heal. The injured bear watched Mudskap lick his wounds with both wonder and a hint of disgust.

Raban put the talon back on his neck and reached out his wing to the cloaked bear.

"Well I apologize for my lack of hospitality, for lack of a better phrase. I only wanted to protect my sister too," Raban said as he motioned over to his sister.

The cloaked bear glanced at Raban's sister and nodded, gesturing for them to sit down together on a nearby boulder.

After they sat down, the bear started. "Of course, I can understand that feeling. I hope you know that I don't blame you or any of your people for her death. I was just caught off guard. I didn't know anyone else was going to be here. My name is Luteo. And it seems like you've met Pern, our warrior," he said as he pointed to the wounded bear. "And here's my other friend," he said, pointing to the darkest bear. "His name is Erem. He's a good friend and wiser than he might look. We've all traveled a long way to get here, and we are all very tired. Do you have any food, by chance?"

"Ka'kaw! Well it is wonderful to meet you, Luteo and your companions. My name is Raban, and this is my sister, Muni. And our little friend over there is Mudskap. We've also traveled a long way and would love to share some of our food with you," Raban said as he walked over to his pack. He came back with three large handfuls of dried Slange meat.

"Why, thank you! I've only seen these creatures in trees. It will be a treat to eat them," said Luteo, as he passed back some meat to his friends.

They all sat there in relative silence as the three bears scarfed down the dried serpent meat and slurped down the lake water. They commented on how delicious this bird food was and Raban promised that after this journey, he would take them back to Arbornesta and show them how to hunt their own Slange.

Raban looked at Pern's healing leg. Mudskap had worked his froggy magic on it. The wound had stopped bleeding and was already fusing back together.

"Hey, Pern, I'm really sorry about attacking you. I promise, I'm not usually like that."

"Well I hope that's not completely true. Because now that we are friends, I want you to protect me the way that you protected against me," Pern said with a wide, goofy smile. "You scared me and you're only half my size." Muni laughed so hard that she spit Slange meat out her beak.

"Fair point! This talon has been handy in quite a few ways on this journey."

As he stepped away from Pern, a whizzing sound flew past Raban's head. He turned around and realized an arrow had just shot by his head and almost hit Pern, landing near the lake. It came from a dense part of the surrounding forests.

"Only a warning shot!" An unknown voice called out, in the same area of the trees. "I didn't mean to shoot it that close! I'm still trying to figure out how to use this bow."

Raban looked over at Luteo, and he nodded. They were already on the same team.

"Please come out and talk to us. We have no ill intent towards you either. Let us speak in peace." called Luteo.

After a few moments of silence, three featherless, hairless creatures stepped forward out of the woods. From their appearance, Raban thought they had to be humans. The man in front was carrying a bow, and the other two, a man and a woman, were carrying large swords and walking towards them.

"We are here on a mission, and we have never seen your types before," the man in front said, eyeing the group up and down. "I'm really sorry about that bow shot! We come from far away and were told that we were going to meet some others here. I just wasn't expecting to see creatures—ahem—I mean, other folks quite like you."

"Well I'm sorry for any confusion. I guess we were not expecting your type either. Are you friend or foe? And what exactly are you?" responded Luteo with a soft quizzical smile.

The man holding the bow started to talk to the other man in a language that no one seemed to understand. After a few minutes of chatting, they both signaled to the woman, and all of them sheathed their weapons at the same time.

"Sorry if we scared you coming out of the forests with all those weapons and shooting bows," said the man in the back, who had just sheathed his sword. "We are not usually like this. We are not warrior people. We are humans from the other side of the mountains, near the coast. Our apologies for the dramatic entrance." The man walked over to the group. "My name is Naka. These two are my friends, Kane and Sumato, and it's an honor to meet you all. To answer your question, I think we are all going to be friends."

Luteo stepped forward, his hairy body shadowing over the small frame of Naka. He sized up his new acquaintance, and after a few tense moments, he laughed and opened his arms to offer a hug. Naka looked back at his two friends and, with some hesitation, stepped into the bear arms. Luteo picked him up and squeezed with a hearty chuckle.

"Welcome to this mysterious group! If you don't know why we are here or what we are doing, then you are one of us!" Luteo said with an unabashed smile as he put Naka back on the ground. In doing so Naka's long sword slipped out of its sheath and fell to the ground.

"Hey," Erem started, stepping quickly forward. "Can I see that weapon?"

Naka looked back at his friends again as if to discuss the matter. They nodded.

"This is my katana; my aunt gave it to me before I left. It is one of the sharpest blades that my people know how to make," said Naka as he handed his blade over to Erem.

"It's beautiful, and as I suspected, it is also marked." Erem walked over to the others showing them the hilt of the sword. Carved into the handle was a red sun symbol. It matched the others perfectly.

"Well it's clear that we've all been chosen to be here." said Raban as he stepped forward, carrying his marked talon in his outstretched wings.

The humans stared at his talon and his wings.

"Can your people fly? We've heard tell of your people, but I've never met anyone like you," asked the light skinned girl, Sumato. She was staring at Muni's feathers.

"We can only glide, but our bird ancestors could fly far distances. After we merged with you, humans, things changed. I've never met a full human like you, but I've seen what some of our people do to emulate you, like farming and cooking. Do your people farm or cook?"

Naka looked surprised. "Of course, we farm! Farming is an essential part of our society. I'm a rice farmer back in my land. Have you ever eaten rice before?"

"My people mostly live in trees, but no I haven't, what is rice? What does it taste—"

"Hey friends, we have company!" called Mudskap, hopping towards the water and pointing to a small boat that was drifting across the lake. Its white sails billowed in the light mountain breeze. Three cloaked figures of various sizes stood at its stern. As it drifted closer to the rocky shore, the tallest robed figure stepped into the water and pulled the boat ashore with ease. The other two hopped off onto land.

The smallest figure stepped towards the group and pulled down his cloak. His skin looked much like the girl in Naka's party. He had short black hair, and heavy-set eyelids. He smiled weakly to the group.

"Greetings, fellow travelers. Whether you know it or not, you are on a very important mission that has been in the works for many years. You all are a part of something much larger than yourselves today. My name is Gaido, and I've been a member of the Resistance for over thirty-five seasons, watching over these parts. These other two are my partners: first, Dalli, my Ursa friend."

The larger cloaked figure pulled back his robe to reveal a furry head with two round thick ears. His black eyes looked like sunken little stones on a brown hairy hill. He smiled and bowed to the crowd.

"The other one is my winged friend, Corvo."

From under the thin cloak, the bird's Corvidean beak protruded. He peeled it back to reveal a narrow and sharp face. His head feathers stuck up in a grey puff.

"Ka'kaw!" Corvo cried as he also bowed towards the crowd.

Gaido continued. "Thank you all for coming and meeting us here. I see that you all have become acquainted and I look forward to learning more about you on our little journey, but I thought it would best to give you some backstory for why you were all sent here." He cleared his throat.

"Three of those standing here have been given marked items that represent their destiny to come to this lake. Can those three people step forward?"

Naka, Luteo, and Raban all stepped towards the robed figures.

"Thank you for coming again and thank you for bringing your friends. This quest will not be achieved without community and trust. Everyone here has a different skill to offer us. You three were chosen by both the Resistance and by Fate, itself, to end the Great Conspiracy that has taken over our land. For many years, we've had to stand by and watch as injustice grew and spread across Godsdorf. All of the pain and suffering spawned in different parts of this land, but it all stemmed from this place." He pointed back at Mt. Vesus. The sun had begun to set behind it, casting a dark shadow over its face.

"Inside of this great majestic mountain lies a fountain of deceit and intrigue. It is created and sustained by powerful leaders from each of your community. You may even recognize some of them. It is your duty now to come with us and confront these tricksters who plot and scheme to hold our societies back. It will be your duty to decide what to do with them. We leave that all up to you. We are only the guides." Gaido stated, looking back at his two partners.

"Tonight, we will head up the mountain. I recommend that you all build a fire and rest up. There will be trials and tribulations ahead for each and every one of you. You are the chosen few, and three of you are the Chosen Ones. The Resistance and the future of Godsdorf depends on your strength and courage. If this pressure is too much, you may leave now, but if you stay, you must see it through. Are you with us?"

Raban scanned the ground. The bears were the first to step forward.

"We are with you and support this mission. Even though I'm young, I've seen enough unnecccooary pain," said Luteo with tears in his eyes. "I will give it my all, and I know my Ursa brothers will too." He pulled his dark special cloak tight around his chest.

Pern and Erem nodded, both holding their staffs in the air behind Luteo. Their eyes betrayed their outward confidence.

Naka spoke to his friend, Kane, again, in their secret language, and both nodded. They stepped forward next with Sumato towards the cloaked guides.

"We might be farmers, but we came here to help our people back home in the midst of revolution. We want to protect our people. Our families have risked everything to help us get here, and we are willing to risk it all for them too. We will do whatever it takes!" cried Naka, with his katana raised. The other two nodded holding their weapons tightly and awkwardly.

Muni stepped forward next. Her talons were shaking.

"My brother has risked everything to bring me here with him. While it might be nice to rest by this lakeside, I know it is not in our blood to let others go on an adventure without tagging along. We are with all of you... right Raban?"

Raban's wings tensed up, but he nodded. One last mission, and then they would finally be free.

"Thank you all for your agreement," Gaido declared as he turned away with the other two cloaked guides. "After the sun is under the horizon, we will start up the mountain and from there, the truth and magnitude of this Great Conspiracy will reveal itself. For now, enjoy your relaxation by the lake. We will gather you when it's time to go."

After they left, Mudskap hopped forward.

"I'm ready to help as well, but first, I think you tall folks should work on making that fire, so we can have one tasty meal before we go. What do you think?"

Luteo laughed and picked up Mudskap.

"I agree with this little guy. Let's enjoy these last moments of freedom with the finest fire and the finest meal that Godsdorf has ever seen!"

The Chosen II

They waited with bated breath as the last rays of sunlight burst through the tree canopies in the lower reaches of the valley. The mood had grown somber once the gravity of the situation fully realized itself. The sun was halfway through its descent in the west, gilding the companions in varying shades of gold and yellow. Kane paced around the smoldering embers of the campfire, meditating in silence as he counted the seconds pass. Naka sat by the fire and whittled a stick while looking lazily at his best friend, tracing his movements with a sullen stare. Luteo sat back with a full belly and stared at the foreign beings around him—simultaneously interested and disgusted in the naked forms of the Humans and the feathered heads of the Corvideans. In stark contrast, Muni and Sumato had seemingly transgressed race entirely and were trying to mimic Sumato's braids with Muni's head feathers. Pern and Erem ignored the diverse crew around them and focused on gathering their weapons and supplies for the journey ahead.

"It is time," Gaido murmured from beneath his deep hood. The three guides rose to their feet as the final glimmer of the sun dissolved. "Gather your belongings, chosen."

"Absolutely, milord," Mudskap intoned with a thick helping of sass. "I sure feel like we're getting bossed around a lot by the ones who are supposed to be leading us."

"Shush, Mudskap." Raban scooped the frog up as he sauntered over to the three elders. "We're as ready as we can be with the little information you've given us." He locked his knee and placed his arms on his hips in expectation.

"We've told you all you need to know. The rest will be learned in time." Dalli spoke in a lazy drawl. Luteo jumped to his feet and hustled towards him.

"How can you expect us to prepare when we don't even know what we're getting into? Are we going to be fighting up there? What are we going to be fighting?" Luteo jabbed with his right claws. Erem walked forward and placed his arm on Luteo's shoulder, in a show of both solidarity and calm. Luteo turned and locked eyes with Erem, deflating his misplaced anger and anxiety.

"I... I'm sorry. We've come so far. I just want to be over with this."

"We've no time to waste. We have many steps ahead of us, and your journey will just be beginning when we arrive." Corvo continued speaking as he turned from the group and faced the mountain. In unison, the three elders fell into single file and marched without checking to see if the group behind them followed.

Naka stepped forward and addressed the group.

"We don't have a choice, do we? It's either follow them up the volcano or stay here and miss our chance." Raban joined Naka's side and nodded, leaning his polespear against his shoulder and clutching the engraved talon to his chest. "Let's get going before we lose them."

The group collected their packs and belongings and brandished their weapons as they caught up to the slow march of the guides. Erem noticed Muni admiring his pickstaff and handed it to her. She smiled as she reached forward to grab it but turned her smile into a look of shock as the weight of the pickstaff dragged her forward into the dirt. Raban chuckled under his breath as he pulled her to her talons, picking Erem's weapon up.

"A heavy weapon you've got there, Ursa," Raban stated as he handed the weapon back to Erem. "Any use when facing something a little more... speedy?"

Erem's voice rumbled in a deep chuckle.

"It is as speedy as I need it to be, Master Corvidean," Erem replied with a slight twinkle in his eye. Raban grinned in return and exclaimed, "Ka'kaw!"

The first stars were beginning to shine through the dark navy sky above when the group burst through the tree line to begin their ascent on bare rock. A chorus of heavy breathing echoed off the stone escarpment that framed their way up the mountain. Despite the thin air and the cold wind whipping across their line, the group had stripped their outer layers to cool off. The guides' pace was slow but steady, and it did not ease when they hit the steep slopes of the volcano. Luteo peered forward past the line, trying to pick out the path upon which Dalli was leading them, but was unable to pick out anything from the craggy rocks ahead.

Dalli made a sharp turn a few paces later into a hidden alcove that was invisible from any vantage point lower in elevation. One by one, the individuals in the line disappeared as they slid into the thin crack that stretched a head higher than Erem—the tallest in their cohort. Luteo was the last to step into the crevice and found himself blind and blundering in the darkness next to Erem and Pern. As his eyes adjusted, he made out a thin hallway stretching into the mountain side, sloped ever so slightly downward.

Corvo waited at the head of the line and allowed time for their eyes to adjust in the dusk. Dalli and Gaido stood next to Corvo and faced the group, then fell into a deep bow.

"This is where we leave you, friends. Our time in this story has come to pass, and we cannot venture deeper into the haven of deceit below." Gaido spoke in a soft whisper, just loud enough for the group to hear.

"There will be a final hurdle that only the seal-bearers can tackle. You will need to leave behind those you love, to save them and the places you know as home."

"What do you mean?" Sumato questioned as she stepped forward. "How are we to know where to go?"

"The path before you will be clear now," Corvo answered. "When you find the golden archway, the chosen must venture forth." He raised his wing and stepped back to allow the cohort to pass. Silence answered his statement. After a few moments of anticipation, Muni took a step forward.

"Well what are we waiting for?" she said quietly. Raban placed his arm on her shoulder and turned his gaze to the rest of the group, lingering on each pair of eyes for a few moments.

"Let's do it," Naka uttered as his somber face hardened. He drew his katana from his hip, the red sun embossed on the hilt. Luteo grinned in the dusk and wrapped his cloak taut over his bulky frame.

Naka led the way past the guide, pausing for a moment to bow before continuing past into the darkness below. The motley procession of folks, all shapes and sizes, followed suit. Raban brought up the rear and paused for a moment once he passed the elders. He turned back to face them, his eyes shining.

"Thank you for your guidance, Masters. I certainly hope there is a reason for all this secrecy..." Raban trailed off, half waiting for a response and half knowing that his words would be unanswered. The guides stayed silent, and Raban turned back to catch up to his friends.

The pathway into the bowels of the volcano lessened in slope the further they descended—a few minutes had passed before the hall evened out and narrowed. Naka was able to pass unhindered, but Erem and Luteo were forced to turn to their sides to press further into the mountain. Naka saw a light glimmering a few paces ahead and whispered in a soft voice to those following.

"I see a light ahead," Erem said, brandishing his pickstaff. "Be prepared for whatever could be waiting for us." Raban gripped his polespear tightly. Naka placed his finger to his lips and shushed to silence his friends.

Naka poked his head from the crevice and was surprised to see a well-lit and furnished hallway that was perpendicular to their unconventional entryway. Candles were mounted in wall lamps that lined the curving path, illuminating the rolling carpet and side tables that appeared every few paces. There was nobody in sight.

"What do you see?". Kane whispered behind his best friend.

"There's nobody here. It's an empty hallway but it looks well-traveled. We should move quickly," Naka replied as he shimmied from the crack into the hallway. Kane's head appeared in the hallway, followed by his body as he trailed Naka. Naka kept watch while the rest of the group moved into the hallway. The Ursa required some pulling and pushing as their frame was almost too bulky to pass through the crack.

"Well? Which way do we go?" asked Mudskap from Raban's shoulder. "It seems like we're presented with two options."

"We could split up?" Pern posited. "Actually, I take it back, we should really stick together. Splitting up doubles our chances of getting caught in here."

"I agree with Pern." Luteo said. "Let's just pick a direction and see if we can find something. If not, we'll turn around and stay together." The group nodded in agreement and followed Luteo's lead as he turned to the right.

The hallway continued for a few hundred paces. The candles were still lit, and furniture still bracketed the path. Sumato startled when Luteo raised his furry arm without speaking and pointed ahead. On the left side of the hallway was a wooden door hewn into the solid rock. The group spread out to surround the doorway, waiting in silence in case anything opened the door. Kane held out his hand as he grasped the door handle, counting down from three on his fingers. Three. Muni held her staff up and supported it with her waist. Two. Erem slung his pickstaff from his shoulder and raised it high above his head. One. Naka pointed the tip of his katana downward to prepare to pull it up in a preemptive strike.

Kane kicked open the door and surged into the room. The small chamber was well-lit, and Kane immediately picked out the lounging figures on his left side. Despite being Ursa, Human, and Corvidean, they were all garbed in similar armor that shimmered underneath the candle-light. The closest guard was frozen and Raban took advantage of his sloth, slicing him from ear to ear with his talon. The other guards jolted into position at the slight of the crimson spray, picking up their swords and spears as they fell back into a defensive huddle.

Luteo charged forward, raising his staff high above his head and slamming it into the shoulder of the closest guard. The human spun backwards, his body crumpling under the force of Luteo's blow. A Corvidean guard lunged forward, taking advantage of Luteo's open flank. Erem's pickstaff blocked the blow just in time, giving Luteo enough space to turn on his heel and crush the Corvidean's knee. The guard keeled over as he lost balance, and Naka finished the skirmish with a downward slice into the Corvidean's neck.

The last two guards pulled backwards, holding swords and shields in a tight formation. Kane, Sumato, and Pern moved into the room and spread out around the guards, cornering them into the tight section of the room. The Ursa guard on the left turned his gaze from Pern and Luteo to Kane and Raban, unable to determine where the next strike would come. The

Human guard on the right seemed more calm and poised. Naka studied his form, trying to deduce why this Human seemed to be devoid of fear or worry at his impending doom. The reason became clear when the Human raised a small circular device to his lip and blew.

Two screeching bursts of noise echoed throughout the room as the Human guard raised the alarm on their intrusion. Muni has pulled her bow from her pack and let fly an arrow but was too late – the guard managed to get off a few more whistles before they silenced him. As the Human slumped backwards against the wall, his Ursa companion threw his shield to the ground and roared with all his might. Lunging forward towards Kane, the Ursa reached with both claws flashing in the candle-light. A sickening squelching sound interrupted his assault, as Raban gutted the Ursa with a deft slice of his talon. The guard fell to the floor in a puddle of guts and blood.

The group waited in silence, breathing heavily after dispatching the guards. While nobody had said it yet, each was listening with all their might to hear if their intrusion had been detected. The silence passed for a few moments, and then a few more, without being broken. Luteo started to let out a deep sigh of relief when a soft whistle echoed from the hallway outside. They had been discovered.

Surveying the room, Raban noted the ornate door on the far side of the room that the guards had been occupying. Intricate gilded creatures lined the archway above the door.

"Look, there. I think that way is how we find the truth in these halls." Raban pointed with his wing, pacing towards the door. "I think that this is the door that Gaido and Corvo were talking about."

"We don't have much time left. The guards are coming for us." Luteo turned back to the group and gestured to the door through which they had entered. "If you hurry, you'll be able to get out of here before the rest of them show up." Pern snorted and Erem shook his head.

"We will not run, Luteolus," Erem said in a slow and steady voice. "We will stay here and delay their entrance as long as we can. They will not expect us, nor our defense of this room, and we will give you the time you need to resolve this. I remember the deep crimson of the sun, on that first morning of the Liberalia. This is larger than us."

Muni ran to the front of the group and jumped into Raban's wings.

"Goodbye, brother. Stay safe in there. I can't lose you." Muni's eyes welled with tears. Raban kneeled and placed Muni on the floor. He hugged her with all his might and looked her right in the eyes with both wings resting on her shoulders.

"Muni, you need to get out of here." Raban looked up at the others and pleaded with his eyes. "Will one of you take her out of here?"

"No!" Muni yelled and brushed his wing off her shoulder. "I will stay here and fight with the rest of them." Muni rubbed the tears from her eyes with the back of her wing. Erem stepped forward.

"Do not worry, Raban," Erem said. "We will take care of Muni. I will die before I let anyone hurt her." He crossed his pickstaff over his heart.

Raban smiled with gratitude and stared at Muni. They locked eyes and were silent for many moments, before Raban nodded and wiped a sole tear from his cheek. He drew Muni in and hugged her, then rose to his feet and looked to Luteo and Naka.

"Naka " Kane stepped forward and paused. "Our parents would be so proud to see where we are today. You need to get to the bottom of this for our village—for our people." Kane hugged Naka and pulled back with his arm on Naka's shoulder.

Naka drew his katana from its sheath and tightened his grip, nodding back to the two other chosen ones. Luteo checked his cloak clasped around his neck, and then held his staff across his chest. Raban put his hand over the talon around his neck and rested his polespear over his shoulder. Ursa, Human, and Corvidean stood together before the gilded door that led to the truth beyond. They turned back to their friends and smiled, then opened the door.

The Chosen III

After the towering doors swung shut, the three figures stopped to take stock of their new surroundings. They had entered a long, wide hallway extending in front of them for what looked like a hundred yards. Candelabras mounted to the walls every few feet illuminated the space just enough to see where they were going, but the light cast a dim, dark mood over the hall. Once he had caught his breath, Naka turned to Raban.

"I'm sorry you had to leave your sister behind. Her name is Muni, right?"

Raban, still panting, nodded his head.

"She will be safe with our friends," Luteo added. "Plus, I saw her out there. Looked like she could handle herself just fine with that staff. During the battle I saw her fight off a soldier by herself with that staff of hers."

"And now it falls to us to see out the end of this grand plan we've been handed," Raban said, nodding. "Thank you both for your kind words. Fortunately or not, I don't have time to think long about how my sister might be faring out there. I will have to trust her word that she can handle herself. Now, we need to figure out our plan for how we will beat whatever waits for us at the end of this hallway. So, let's go over what we know of what to expect."

"Not nearly enough," Naka stated. "Those robed guides of ours haven't exactly been fountains of information. We know that we're interrupting some kind of meeting of powerful figures of our societies. I don't know about you two, but for my people that could be anyone from a governor or supreme magistrate up to Empress Karuto herself."

"So," Luteo replied. "Our priority should be collecting as much information as we can, as quietly as we can. We have the element of surprise—so far as we know—and we should keep it that way until we have any idea of what's going on."

Naka nodded. "Leave this hallway as quietly as possible and figure out what we can. Works for me. In case we open those doors and find ourselves face to face with a dozen armed guards, though, what are you guys working with, weapon-wise? I saw your staff in action, Luteo, and I saw you with that long spear you carry, Raban. Anything else we can take advantage of? As for myself, I have only this sword with me."

"Just the staff for me," Luteo said. "No hidden weapons. My cloak is more powerful than it looks, though—it's completely impervious to cutting or stabbing."

"Well then remind me to stand behind you at all times. Raban?"

"Along with my polespear I also have the talon around my neck. It may look ceremonial, but it carries a sharp edge to it. And I have poison throwing darts."

"Those darts certainly sound useful," Naka chuckled. "I'm glad you let us know about them. Is the poison fast-acting?"

"As fast-acting as poisons come," Raban said through a grin. "If worst comes to worst and we blow our chance at surprise, I can try to hit as many of them as I can right away. Whoever they are."

"Ok, let's make that plan C if all hell breaks loose," Luteo answered. "If we get discovered, I think we should try to stall first for as long as possible to get more information out of whoever's out there. But let's try to remain undiscovered, first."

Naka and Raban nodded. "Alright. Are you two ready?" Naka asked.

"As ready I can be," Luteo replied.

"Same," said Raban.

The three of them walked down the hall, careful with their steps and soft spoken with the few words they needed to say. As they approached the end of the hallway, they slowed even further and spoke in hushed whispers. "Okay," Naka said. "I suppose now we should try to open these huge doors as slowly as we can and hope they're the kind of huge doors that don't make noise, as opposed to all the other huge doors I've seen in my life that cause a commotion. No sweat."

The three of them pushed on the right-hand door slowly at first so as not to raise suspicion. They let out silent sighs of relief when the door did not let out a noise, allowing them enough space to move through the doorway and close the door without letting out so much as a squeak. The room they now found themselves in dwarfed the hallway they exited from in both area and volume, although not in length. Yards in front of them stood eight large, ornate Corinthian columns in a perfect circle that held up a painted ceiling depicting dozens of images of the Corvideans, the Ursa, and Humanity. Many of the images showed all three races together, fighting each other in bloody battles.

In the middle of the room, right in the center of the circle of columns, stood seven hooded figures. The figures varied in height and size, but each wore the same style of white robes, tailored perfectly to the form of its owner. The floor beneath them bore an intricate patterned design, with black stone cutting throughout the otherwise white marble surface, but if the pattern meant anything, Naka did not recognize it. In the middle of the standing figures sat a large table, which came up to the ribs of the shortest of them. Candelabras like the ones in the hallway perched on the columns fifteen or so feet above the floor and provided the main source of light in the room. Luckily for Luteo, Raban, and Naka, the outer edges of the room had very few light sources, which helped disguise their presence from the cultish gathering, in addition to the fact that the hooded figures seemed too focused on the matters at hand in the middle of the room to pay much attention to the outskirts of the room.

The three would-be interlopers found a decorative slab of marble to hide behind near the entrance to the hallway. From their hiding spot, they could only just make out the faces of half of the circle. From where they stood, the three of them could make out two Corvideans, three Ursa, and two figures facing away from them that had the height and proportions of Humans. Luteo and Raban both let out extremely faint, although still audible, gasps that forced them to cover their mouths as Naka gave each of them sharp looks.

"What is it?" Naka whispered, as quietly and clearly as he could manage.

Raban spoke first, in a hushed and serious tone. "I know those beaks. That's great leader Vali and Lord Chasta. Vali leads the tree folk where I come from and Chasta leads the city folk. I've never seen them together before—I've never even heard of them interacting. Their people are rivals of one another. Our ways of life are hardly compatible. Vali sent me to kidnap Lord Chasta's niece after Chasta's goons kidnapped and hurt my sister."

"And those are the three Denmasters of my people," uttered Luteo. "Bern, Arcus, and Kira. I thought they only came together for the Liberalia once a year. Our kind rarely speak to bears of other kingdens. We compete in every way you could imagine. And it's not exactly a friendly competition. I'm from Bern's kingden, and Arcus' son tried to kill me on my way here."

"I see," said Naka. "I can't tell who those Humans are from here but given the high stature of the representatives from your societies, I'd be willing to bet the shorter one is Empress Karuto. She leads the entirety of Sokoku, and her rule is what my father and the people of my village back home are fighting against. My father and my aunt must have sent me here to stop her."

"And the other Human?" asked Raban. "Do you know who that might be?"

"I'm not sure. No one in my society rivals the Empress. It could be a guard of hers. Whenever I've heard news of her travels in Sokoku, I always hear of her contingent of bodyguards."

"So," Luteo offered. "The leaders of our respective societies are meeting secretly inside of a mountain, far away from each of our homes. The hooded elders who sent us from our homes to this mountain clearly do not get along with these hooded elders that rule over us. Where does that leave us? Are we meant to fight these people?"

"This doesn't make sense," Raban said, stroking the feathers under his beak. "These leaders of ours have essentially isolated their entire societies from one another and yet they meet here?"

The leaders began uttering a low hum that echoed heavily throughout the chamber. They slowly raised their hands straight out from their bodies as they hummed until their arms and wings reached about a forty-five-degree angle from their torsos. Then, the shorter Human spoke. Her voice was low for a Human woman and cut clearly through the room. "It is time. Now that we have all gathered here, let us begin the two-hundredth meeting of the Order."

The other hooded gatherers nodded their agreement. "Now," the white bear with dark rings circling his eyes said, "As a first order of business, I believe you have a pressing topic to you'd like to discuss, Karuto."

The woman facing away from the three of them nodded. "Yes, Arcus, thank you. As you all know, there's been an irritating little peasant rebellion in the boondocks of Sokoku in a little nothing village called Manaolana." The hairs on the back of Naka's neck bristled at her disdain for his home. "Somehow, despite all odds, these Nakai peasants have managed to convince some of their bedfellows to follow their lead. The revolution is spreading across the coast, I'm afraid. We have soldiers stationed and ready to fight, of course, but we'd rather not incite an all-out war."

"And what do you ask of the Order?" asked Lord Chasta.

"We ask for supplies," replied the Empress. "We have the means to crush their rebellion outright, of course. We could root out every whisper of insolence in every village, but that would waste resources better spent on other, more impactful work. With the proper tools we could instead make an example of the epicenter of the revolt, this tiny Manaolana. We could wipe it off the map and let all the other villages know the price of betrayal in Sokoku."

At the Empress' words Naka's face flushed with anger and he had to grit his teeth till his gums turned white to avoid shouting out at her.

Arcus responded first. "My clan has a guild of fire blowers that would be happy to burn down every last home in that village, if given the word."

Lord Chasta spoke up next. "We city-dwelling Corvideans have a legion of cavalry trained to ride five-horned rhinoceroses into battle. I'm sure whatever small force these villagers have dredged up would fall quite easily to my mounted soldiers." He smiled. "It's been too long since we've had an opportunity to use them to their fullest potential. I would quite like the chance to watch them tear those wretched people limb from limb."

"Then it is settled," stated the Empress.

"Not quite," the stout, bookish Denmaster to Arcus' left chimed in. "I have to wonder, Empress, why you think a small rebellion that you say you can control on your own is reason enough to risk revealing the link between our societies. When word of rhinoceros-riding Corvideans and flame-spewing Ursa fighters reaches the cities of Humanity, will the people in those cities not wonder how it is that their government enlisted the help of two societies that before that point had rarely interacted with their kind? This plan seems to come dangerously close to suggesting that perhaps our societies are not better off in isolation after all."

"A fair point, Denmaster Kira," said Vali, the tall bird next to Lord Chasta. "I have to admit, I'm not surprised at this revolution. This is what happens when one half of your society exerts complete dominance over the other. We Corvideans have tricked our people so thoroughly into fighting the opposing side that neither party has a revolt to stage among their own kind. Even the bears have done this with their three, more-or-less evenly matched Kingdens. But I digress. Empress, how do you imagine you will deal with the rumors of our help?"

The Empress replied to this question through pursed lips. "There will not be any rumors to deal with if there are no witnesses to share their version of events. My soldiers will encircle Manaolana and ensure that no people get into or out of the village for miles. Once our troops have the area around the village secure, we can sail your fire breathers and rhinos into the village itself and tear it to pieces. If we leave none alive, the rumors will still grow to outlandish proportion, but they will deal in so many different versions of events that no one will know what to think. The mystery surrounding the elimination of this cesspool of a village will dissuade the others. Those inclined to revolt will feel helpless in their confusion and their imaginations will keep them from picking up arms for generations." It took everything Naka could muster not to stand up right then, but Raban and Luteo placed their hands on his shoulders to calm him.

"And what if these rebels see the attack coming and retreat?" Asked Kira. "Your coastal land has many nooks and crannies to hide insurgent fighters for a long, long time."

"We have seen to it that the rebels will do no such thing," said a voice strangely familiar to Naka. "Manaolana is their base of operations, the spiritual heart of their rebellion. Even the very name means 'hope' in the Nakai language. They will not abandon it. Besides, they think they have an ally in me. I can steer them in whatever direction I choose, including to stay put in their village."

All at once, the realization of where he had heard that voice before hit Naka like a coconut from the top of a palm tree. "That gods-damned traitor!" Naka whispered in as harsh and quiet a tone as he could muster. He could barely contain his shock and rage. "Waiwai Kamoi. The richest Nakai in Sokoku is in league with these people. He's working with the Empress." Naka turned to Luteo and Raban. "I met him on my way to the mountain. He promised to aid my father's rebellion and thought he'd sent me back to bring word to my father, but I came here first."

"I think we've heard enough," Raban clucked. "They've been plotting with each other and keeping our societies apart for who knows how long. Now they plan to eradicate an entire village just to hold onto their power. How should we strike?"

Luteo replied, "There are seven of them and three of us. Whatever plan we try, we need to take full advantage of the surprise of our attack. Raban, how many do you think you could hit with your poison darts if you were to start throwing out of the blue?"

"Before they got wise and took themselves out of my line of sight? No more than two from here. I'm good, but they're fairly far away and those pillars make for great cover."

Luteo nodded. "Leaving us with five. Not great, but depending on who we can hit, far greater than having to face seven. Arcus, the one with rings around his eyes, is the biggest threat. If we can, we need to take him out first."

"What if I could lure them away from the middle of the room and closer to our position without revealing you two?" Naka asked.

"And what do you propose?" said Raban. "Don't get yourself killed out there."

"As long as they think it's just me in this room they won't feel the need to attack immediately. I'll go out and confront Waiwai and the Empress and try to draw some of the others out from the cover of the columns. Wait for my signal to throw a poison dart at Arcus, and after you hit him try to hit as many others as you can."

Luteo and Raban nodded and remained still behind the slab of marble while Naka walked out at an angle between the hallway's entrance and the circle of columns. When he reached a far enough distance out to the side of the marble slab, he spoke.

"You're right, Waiwai." He used as confident and commanding a voice as he could find within him. The circle of Order members nearly broke their necks in their hurry to turn around and identify the new voice. Waiwai had such shock on his face that Naka nearly grinned. "We did think you were on our side. A mistake we shall not make again. How could you betray your people? What does it take for a Nakai to turn against his own?"

The Empress laughed. "My, my. We appear to have our very own rabble-rouser in our midst. My dear," she said to Naka. "It takes nothing more than wealth for a Nakai to turn against his own. Why would Waiwai risk the fortune he's managed to amass within the rules of our society for some village farmer's foolish pipedream of a freer society?"

"How did you get here?" Waiwai finally spouted. "Did you follow me all the way here?"

"Oh, I followed you alright." Naka lied through his teeth. "You were quite easy to follow as you don't move very quickly now that you're rich and fat."

"Enough," Arcus asserted. "Boy, what are you doing here? What do you hope to achieve barging into this room? Do you honestly think you have a prayer of escaping?"

"Big words from an ugly bear," Naka replied. "Now that I can see you clearer up close, you look like even less of a threat."

Arcus bristled with anger. He puffed out his chest instinctively and a pang of fear went through Naka's spine that he hoped none of the others could see. Arcus thundered toward Naka and stopped a few yards away from him to let out a bellowing roar.

"All bark and no bite," Naka goaded. "Watch yourself, you overgrown raccoon."

Arcus roared once more and started to run toward Naka at full sprint. Naka drew his sword and saw a flash of shining metal fly out from his peripheral vision to hit the Denmaster in the throat. Arcus' momentum carried him halfway to Naka before he fell flat on his face at Naka's feet. Naka looked to the side to see Raban standing out from behind the marble hideaway in the motion of throwing a second poison dart. He took aim at Denmaster Bern, but the projectile glanced harmlessly off one of the columns in the center of the room.

The other Order members hid instinctively behind their nearest pillars. Before Raban could throw his next dart, a stone flew from Vali's sling and hit the young Corvidean squarely in his throwing shoulder, knocking him down. Kira and Bern took the opportunity to charge toward Naka, who held his sword as firmly as he could as he braced for combat. Just before the Ursa reached Naka, Luteo ran out from behind the marble slab and tackled Denmaster Bern to the ground. Naka dove to the side to avoid Kira's charge and got to his feet as quickly as he could.

"Raban!" shouted Naka. "You good?"

"Yeah, I'll be fine," said Raban. "Let's kick their fucking asses. Ka'kaw!"

Raban ran out from around the pillar toward Naka and reached him as Kira came around for another swing. Raban pulled out his polespear and twirled it above his head before stepping out with his feet to assume a fighting stance. Naka, not knowing any moves, held his sword firmly in his grasp. Kira ran at them at full sprint, holding a large wood club at his side. Before Kira came into striking distance with his club, Raban stepped to the side and jabbed Kira in the thigh with the polespear, causing him to tumble to the ground. Naka then ran up to Kira and slashed at his prone body, slicing diagonally across his back. Kira roared in pain but swung his club back at Naka's feet and knocked Naka's legs out from under him. Naka fell to the ground clutching his left ankle. Raban came up behind Kira and stabbed him in the back while Kira started to step to his feet. Kira's body fell to the ground lifeless.

On the ground several feet away, Luteo rolled on the ground with Bern, each attempting to wrest the advantage from the other. Luteo's staff lay out of either's reach. They swapped blow after blow, clawing and punching at each other. Naka and Raban ran over to help Luteo when Lord Chasta and Vali intercepted them. Vali slung another stone, this time toward Naka, and Naka felt the wind from the flying rock as it missed his neck by an inch. Lord Chasta, longsword in hand, sliced at the air before running straight for Raban. As Lord Chasta swung down at him, Raban used the blade of his polespear to parry the blow to the side and punched the lord in the beak.

Naka ran at Vali before Vali had time to load another stone into his sling and cut the weapon from the Corvidean's grasp. He sliced back across Vali's body, but Vali jumped backward to avoid the cut. Vali pulled a dagger out from under his robes and threw it at Naka, who dodged the blade. Naka then charged at Vali and swung down, striking Vali from shoulder toward the middle of his chest. As Vali slumped to his knees, Naka looked down at him, watching the left side of Vali's body separate slightly from the rest of it. When Vali's blood started to seep out from his wound, Naka promptly threw up where he stood.

Luteo now stood opposite Bern as the two circled each other catching their breath. Luteo had picked his staff up from the floor and held it firmly in both hands. Bern carried no visible weapons, but held his hands up in semi-open fists, creating a space to expose his sharp claws. He laughed. "You've come all this way just to die, eh, cub? Are you that eager to meet your sister?"

Luteo could not contain his rage. "You let her die! You got saved up on that stage, but you left Isabell to die!"

"Ay, I got saved." Bern smiled. "Just as I had planned when I ordered that assassination attempt."

Luteo stopped moving and stepped back, shocked. "When you... when you ordered the attempt? You arranged to take your own life?"

"My dear cub," Bern sighed. "I would never aim to take my own life. I'm much too big a fan of me for that. I told Arcus about the plot before the ceremony and made sure he was close enough to knock me out of the bombs' blasts. In my defense, I did not intend for your sister to find herself on the receiving end of the attack, but then again what's one life to give compared to the power and support I wielded after the assassination attempt? I will do more than enough good to outweigh her sacrifice. Your death, on the other hand.... I think I will relish killing you. Although I also must give you thanks—with Arcus dead, I'll be able to swoop in and claim his Kingden for my own."

"Murderer! This one is for my sister. Raban! Now!"

In the middle of his parrying with Lord Chasta, Raban threw a poison dart at the two bears. The dart whizzed past Bern and hit Luteo's cloak in his left shoulder. Luteo fell to the ground, grasping at the dart. Once he'd realized what happened, Bern let out a bellowing laugh.

"Such a fitting end for such an unfortunate example of an Ursa. Say hello to your sister for me, Luteo."

Bern turned away from Luteo's body and started off toward Lord Chasta to help him with Raban. "I believe I owe you thanks, young bird. I would have had that cub, but you've saved me time."

Raban, between parries with Lord Chasta, replied, "oh, don't thank me. I wouldn't count Luteo out just yet." He smiled as he deflected another of Lord Chasta's blows.

Bern turned around, confused. He glanced back just in time to see Luteo's paw jam a poison dart into his upper arm. As Bern fell to the floor, Luteo laughed. "Such a fitting end for such an unfortunate example of a Denmaster. I can't wait to bring your head back to Berarbor." Luteo turned to intercede in Raban and Lord Chasta's duel, swinging his staff down on the city-dweller to give Raban some breathing room. "Raban, I'm going to assume you remembered that my cloak is impervious to blades and not that you accidentally hit me instead of Bern."

"I prefer that assumption," Raban replied. He put his weight on his back leg and pointed his polespear toward Lord Chasta. "Two against one, Chasta. I don't like your odds."

Lord Chasta sighed and gripped his longsword at beak level. "Enough with the quips."

Naka wiped his mouth and started off toward Raban and Bern when he felt a sharp pang in his right shoulder. He glanced down and found a metal blade jutting out of his flesh. Pain tore through him and flooded his brain with signals and alerts, imploring him to stop everything and scream. He looked back at the source of the dagger and found the Empress a few feet behind him, smiling.

"Not bad for an old woman, eh? I've had many years of practice." She took another dagger from her robes and threw it straight into Naka's thigh. He fell to the floor in agony. She walked over to him, a third dagger in hand. "I have to say, I am impressed that you and your band of creatures managed to make it all this way. Just think what you could have accomplished under other circumstances. But you chose this route for yourself, my dear."

She stood tall, gathering herself, and Naka couldn't help but feel impressed by her presence. "Mr. Kamoi, get out from behind that column and pull yourself together. We've overstayed our welcome."

Waiwai grabbed the base of his robes and scurried over to the Empress. "Your majesty, you must go. I shall stay behind and cover your exit."

The Empress rolled her eyes. "Oh please, like you've been any help at all during this mess. We both need to leave. Let Chasta handle the other two himself. You're more useful to me alive and writing banknotes than dead and gathering dust. Now come on."

The two headed to the end of the room on the other side from where Naka, Luteo, and Raban had entered, toward what Naka figured must be another exit of some kind. His shoulder and thigh burning from the two daggers, he let out as loud a shout as he could muster as he stood to his feet.

"Stop where you are! You will be brought to justice for plotting to annihilate the village of Manaolana and murder all of its residents!"

The Empress and Waiwai turned to face him. "Waiwai," the Empress said. "This boy just doesn't know when he's dying, does he?" She went to reach for another dagger when Luteo came running at them and tackled both to the ground. A loud snap let out as the Empress' right knee shattered against the ground. Her scream pierced the air and reverberated across the room. Luteo grabbed his staff and began to swing down at her when Naka shouted out at him.

"No! Leave her alive. She's more useful to us as leverage than dead. I will take her back to Manaolana, so she can answer for her crimes."

Luteo nodded. "And the man too?"

Naka paused for a moment of consideration. "I don't think he needs to be conscious for this."

Waiwai shrieked as he crawled away from Luteo, who picked him up by his collar and slammed him back onto the ground. Waiwai's body went limp instantly, and Naka could not tell for sure whether he had died or had simply lost consciousness.

"Thank you, Luteo." Naka smiled between wheezes. "Now that they can't walk, I think I can take it from here."

Luteo nodded. "Raban still needs my help." He ran back across the room, where Raban spun around and swung at Lord Chasta, who blocked his swing in a flash of sparks. Lord Chasta struck again quickly and knocked Raban's polespear out of his hands and sent it flying out of Raban's reach. Raban stepped back and shifted his weight between his feet to prepare to dodge Chasta's attack. Lord Chasta readied himself for a swing, but instead of aiming at Raban swung out to his side where Luteo approached, slicing open Luteo's forearm. Raban took the opportunity to tear the talon around his neck off its string and drove the razor-sharp talon into Lord Chasta's chest. Lord Chasta stumbled backward, blood spilling out of his mouth as he gasped for air. He looked down at the talon and back up at Raban before falling to the floor.

Raban went to Luteo to make sure his arm was ok before the two rushed over toward Naka. Luteo tore a stretch of cloth off his garb and tied it around Naka's injured thigh. "This will help stop the bleeding," he said gingerly. Here, let me see your shoulder. He tied another stretch over Naka's shoulder and around his armpit, stemming the tide of blood coming out from the wound. The Ursa and the Corvidean brought the Human to his feet and draped his arms over their shoulders. "I can handle his weight," Raban said to Luteo. "Can you get those two?" He gestured to the two Humans lying on the floor a few yards away. After removing any weapons they still had, Luteo picked up the Empress and grabbed Waiwai's body by his feet, and the five of them headed for the door to meet their friends, who were hopefully waiting for them outside.

Epilogue

Raban stood with Muni in disbelief. Looming in front of them was the largest bird that they had ever seen. Its black wing feathers curved down its gigantic body in beautiful layers. Its large obsidian eyes stared right at them. Raban hesitated, but he bowed low towards the giant black bird. When he looked up, he was surprised to see that it was bowing towards him.

He stepped forward and put his hand on its powerful chest, and he could feel its soft purr from below. The bird bent down and pecked at Raban's chest, pulling the large talon necklace forward.

"Ka'kaw, my dearest child, where did you get that talon?" asked the bird in a silvery voice.

"My father gave it to me. I'm not sure where he got it though."

"Yes, of course, passed down to you from your father, and I think we can assume, he received it from his father or mother, and so on and so on. Well, it is quite a beautiful talon, so I can understand why."

Raban felt confused but nodded. Muni stepped up next to him and whispered

"Look at the bird's talons."

Raban looked down and noticed that the black bird was missing one of its massive talons...

"Wait, is this yours?" Raban asked, gesturing towards the talon on his neck.

"Oh no worries, it's yours now. I've lived longer without it than with it at this point. Just keep good care of it. Well, at least better care than I did," the bird chirped with a wide smile. "Has it treated you kindly?" the giant bird asked.

"It has saved my life and my sister! We owe you everything. What is your name?"

"I'm very happy to hear that my children. And I don't know my name, but from what I hear, your people often call me the King Raven, which I find amusing because I'm no king, nor am I even male." The King Raven's eyes sparkled in the sunlight.

Muni giggled.

"We owe you everything, King Raven." Raban prostrated himself on the ground in front of the giant bird.

"Oh stop, and please stand up. You owe yourselves more than you owe me. You owe the friends and strangers that helped you survived your journey. I think you've been away from home long enough. I would love to fly you back to your nest if that's okay with you?"

"We would be most honored, *my Queen Raven!*" squealed Muni with a large smile.

"Ah I like the ring of that name," the black bird said with a nod. "Well get on and hold tight, we have some distance to go."

Muni and Raban scrambled up the back of the bird and gripped onto her thick feathers.

The giant bird stretched out her massive wings, and after only a few flaps, they were airborne. The wind whistled against all of their feathers, and they flew faster and higher. As they rose in the sky, the bird turned her head to look towards them.

"Are you two ready to fly without me?" called the Queen Raven.

"What? No, we can't. We don't have it in us," cried Raban.

"Of course, you can. Whatever a bird can do, you can do, and whatever a human can do, you can do as well. Have you learned anything on your journey? Only you are holding yourself back. Try and see for yourself," called the Queen Raven.

Muni without hesitation let go of the feathers and was flung back in the air. She was flapping her wings but falling.

"Muni!" Raban jumped off the back too, and the wind shot him back towards her. They were both falling but flapping their wings as the wind rushed around them.

Suddenly, he couldn't see Muni! But when he looked up he saw her floating forward, no longer falling...

"I'm flying, Rabe! I'm flying" Raban could hear her muffled calls from above.

She was flying! She pushed her way up and was flying next to the Queen Raven now. He was so distracted by her flight that he had barely noticed that he also stopped falling. He looked at his wings and he was doing it too!

Their journey may have ended, but their lives had just taken flight.

***

Luteo stepped into the sunlight of the Main Square and was overcome by the cacophony of the crowd assembled to meet him. Ursa he had never seen before clamored and pushed to see him, to touch him as he walked towards the stage at the far end of the square. Pern and Erem followed him into the light, standing at his shoulders. Kermodei waited for him, standing with his mother and father, grinning from ear to ear and full of energy that was long forgotten in the years since his youth.

Luteolus ascended the stage and was assaulted by a hug from his mother, grasping at him as if she wasn't sure he was truly there. His father waited patiently, then wiped a tear from his eye as he grabbed his son in a bear hug. Kermodei hung his head in a deep bow, and then turned to face the crowd.

"Today we welcome back three of our brightest stars, our defenders against the insidious rulers that sapped our society like a cancer," Kermodei addressed the crowd, who answered in cheers. "We have a long way to go. We need to figure out the extent of this evil, to root it out and to burn it out. We need to rebuild upon its ashes, to bring seedlings from the fertile soil of rebirth."

Kermodei motioned for Luteo to step forward. Luteo paused, then took his place next to Kermodei. The excited buzz of the crowd rose to a new tenor as he bowed to the Ursa. He motioned for silence and the discord ended.

"I did not do this alone. Pern and Erem, this is your doing just as much as it is mine." Pern and Erem waved in an awkward manor, then stepped back from their place behind Luteo on the stage.

"I did this for Isabell. I did this for you. Never again can we cause such hurt to ourselves, just to further our own agendas and to enrich our families. We must create a system that allows us to monitor our own actions, to bring accountability to our leaders. They may be leaders, but they are also our servants."

The crowd nodded in agreement and waited for Luteo to continue. Instead, Luteo turned back to his family, and motioned for his parents to join him at the front of the stage. They stood beside him, and he spoke for a final time.

"Now we must mourn the loss of my sister. We have made a grave sacrifice for the Ursa, and in turn we must ask for the Ursa to make a great sacrifice for our people. Do not forget that your neighbor is just another version of you. Remember the sins of the parents, and the hurt of the children will pass."

With that, Luteo walked with his family off the stage, and exited the Main Square.

***

Naka sat with Kane at the edge of the wooden dock, their feet dangling in the water. The bright white bandage covering Naka's shoulder contrasted with his tanned skin. Mudskap was able to heal most of the damage done, but Naka's body needed to handle the rest the old-fashioned way. The two had only gotten back to Manaolana two days ago and they had spent nearly every available minute near the water. While they were away in Kalani and at the mountain, their parents had taken the small seedling of a revolution and catalyzed it into the whirling first winds of a storm. The whole village had transformed into a base of operations for the rebellion and people from villages, towns, and even cities had arrived in droves, eager to join the fight.

Naka smiled as he recalled the looks on everyone's faces when they had brought the Empress back in chains. They had taken a longer route back to avoid as many people as they could and had hired a wagon to hide both the Empress and Waiwai, who had survived Luteo's bodyslam more or less intact. They had sent word to Manaolana ahead of them so that their parents could receive them outside of the craziness of the village. When Naka's father first saw the Empress, he didn't realize who it was—not many had seen the Empress in the flesh—but he did recognize Waiwai. He nearly punched Waiwai in the face when he found out about his betrayal of the Nakai rebellion. Waiwai and the Empress were moved to the prison quarters in the village. Land overseers that refused to give in to the rebellion, Boto included, sat in their own cells along with the two high-profile guests behind the same bars that they previously used to punish Nakai that did not meet their standards of obedience. More than two dozen of the most trusted soldiers of the rebellion stood watch over the prisoners at all hours of the night.

Naka and Kane told their parents every detail of their journey and how they had managed to capture both Waiwai and the Empress herself. They explained the secret rendezvous that the two had had with the leaders of the Ursa and the Corvideans and also how they teamed up with a few Ursa and Corvideans to take them all down along the way. The day after the meeting, the leaders of the rebellion sent messages to any contacts they had in the other societies, hoping to bridge the gap that had been established between the societies for nearly two hundred years.

Footsteps sang out on the wooden dock behind them and the two turned to see Sumato walking toward them. "Your parents told me I might find you two here," she said as she sat down between them. She rested her head on Kane's shoulder, who then put his arm around her. They had grown close on the journey back from the mountain, especially after fighting together to keep the guards from catching up to Naka, Luteo, and Raban. Although the thought was highly premature, he couldn't help but hope for the prospect of more half Nakai, half Yamahito children running around the village. Maybe if they fought hard enough to bridge the inequality long established in Sokoku, their movement could eventually bring other people together, too.

STEVIE B. B. KING

ABOUT THE AUTHOR

Stevie B. B. King lives in Seattle, Washington, and enjoys not writing for eleven months of the year. This is their first published work in the United States. Stevie B. B. King is the pen name of Ping Pong Bing Bong (P. P. B. B.) who writes under a pseudonym due to focus group opposition to their name. For the record, Ping Pong is a sport played around the world originating in Victorian England. Bing Bong rhymes with Ping Pong.

Made in the USA
San Bernardino, CA
04 February 2018